A Candlelight Ecstasy Romance®

"YOU POUT WELL," RAFE SAID MISCHIEVOUSLY.

Melissa stared at the handsome man behind the camera. "I'm not pouting."

"Well, whatever you're doing, you're very photogenic. You look as cute as an angry sugar cookie."

"Let's leave out the cute remarks, okay?" Melissa asked.

"What's wrong with cute? It could be just right for the promotion campaign these test shots are for."

"I like to think there are aspects to my personality that are more positive than cute, that's all."

"Well, maybe we can explore those today too." His tone was soft and seductive and Melissa felt her pulse quicken. "Exploring can be very exciting. . . ."

CANDLELIGHT ECSTASY ROMANCES®

MISTLETOE MAGIC

Lynn Patrick

A CANDLELIGHT ECSTASY ROMANCE®

Published by
Dell Publishing Co., Inc.
1 Dag Hammarskjold Plaza
New York, New York 10017

ISBN: 0-440-15635-1

Printed in the United States of America

First printing—December 1985

Thanks to Stacy, Wendy, Kristi, Todd,
and Julie for their naughty inspiration.

Thanks also to Lydia, Kelle, and Maggie,
who have allowed us to share our humor
and fantasy with our readers.

To Our Readers:

We have been delighted with your enthusiastic response to Candlelight Ecstasy Romances®, and we thank you for the interest you have shown in this exciting series.

In the upcoming months we will continue to present the distinctive, sensuous love stories you have come to expect only from Ecstasy. We look forward to bringing you many more books from your favorite authors and also the very finest work from new authors of contemporary romantic fiction.

As always, we are striving to present the unique, absorbing love stories that you enjoy most—books that are more than ordinary romance. Your suggestions and comments are always welcome. Please write to us at the address below.

Sincerely,

The Editors
Candlelight Romances
1 Dag Hammarskjold Plaza
New York, New York 10017

CHAPTER ONE

"Santa Claus has been getting out of line, if you ask me," the elf in the red tunic said. The bells at the end of his peaked cap jingled as he continued emphatically, "We all know his rosy cheeks and nose are a little *too* red. He's been boozing it up on his dinner break." The elf looked around the storage room where Santa's helpers had gathered among cartons of dolls, stuffed animals, games, and other toys.

Another elf, dressed in green, spoke up. "So he has a couple of glasses of wine with his food. He says it helps him feel more jolly. What's the harm?"

"He's jolly all right," complained the reindeer, her large doe eyes blinking indignantly. "He's so jolly he pinched me, right on the—"

"Haunch?" asked the green elf, laughing. "Santa's been bad, for goodness' sake!"

"It's not funny, Terry," said the teddy bear. "Santa's been bothering more than his helpers. I've noticed him giving the eye to passing customers too. Just as I was lining up my camera to take a picture the other day, he winked at a good-looking mother and let her kid fall right off his lap. We're representing Haldan-Northrop here. What kind of image does that kind of behavior present for an elegant Fifth Avenue store? It's downright embarrassing."

"I think we should report him to the promotions director

before one of the customers does," suggested Arlene, the black sugarplum fairy, flouncing her lavender tulle skirts.

Looking from face to disapproving face, Melissa Ryan, the other sugarplum fairy, stepped forward and spoke in her soft, melodic voice. "Wait a minute. Don't you think we should talk to Santa first? After all, Clarence was unemployed for several months before he got this position. It's hard to find jobs in New York. Let's confront him and talk about it. He's usually so good with the children," she pleaded earnestly.

"Clarence means well," Terry said, supporting Melissa. "And he really looks the part. He even grew his own beard for it. I think his flirting problem is due to loneliness and the fact that he's always fancied himself a leading man, although he failed to get those roles in Hollywood or on Broadway. Have a heart, folks. Many of us are unemployed actors here."

"Yeah. We know Clarence is a friend of yours, Terry," grumbled the reindeer, undoing the zipper at the top of her antlered costume. "But something has to be done. Personally, I don't care if you report him or talk to him, but please make a decision and tell me about it tomorrow. My shift is over for today."

"Let's talk to him," Melissa suggested again. "We can all go together."

"Why don't you talk to him?" Arlene asked. "You're the sympathetic one."

"Yes, why don't you?" agreed the teddy bear. "You've got more time. I've got to get my camera equipment ready."

Terry turned to Melissa. "Clarence is my friend, but I think you might be able to handle him better," he said.

"Okay. So it's agreed," chimed in the red elf. "Melissa's going to talk to Clarence and if he doesn't shape up then we go to the promotions director."

As the group walked out of the room to the department-store floor, Melissa followed last, wondering how she had once again managed to place herself in a difficult situation. Why did it have to be she who had to talk to Santa? Could she make Clarence understand? She supposed it was worth a try. Although she'd known him for only a short time, she felt sorry for the older man. And talking to him as soon as possible was the only right thing to do. Well, she guessed she'd just have to give herself credit for being a "good fairy."

Skirting the sign before Santa's chair that stated he would be back at 6 P.M., she glanced at the photographer as he set up his equipment. The teddy bear had removed the paws of his costume to fiddle with his camera. A small boy and his adult escort were watching the proceedings, and when the child looked Melissa's way, she gave him a radiant smile. The boy's eyes grew wide with wonder. She knew he was impressed by her magical appearance. Well, at least she'd found one perfect part-time job for a five-foot-one-inch woman—not that she'd admit to being less than five feet two. Everyone insisted that, with her long flaxen curls and fragile features, Melissa looked like a real, honest-to-goodness fairy.

Deciding to go to the store's business offices and look for Clarence, Melissa stepped onto a nearby escalator, carefully placing her ballet-slippered feet in the very center of a moving step. Then she adjusted her pink bespangled tulle skirts and pulled in her stiff net and wire wings to avoid the handrails swiftly gliding by. The costume wasn't easy to walk around in since it caught on things so readily.

Disembarking on the upper floor, she inquired after Clarence, hoping she'd be able to find him, as usual, visiting with the attractive secretaries at the end of his break. Unfortunately, no one had seen him today. Feeling concerned and disappointed, Melissa quickly headed back downstairs. She would have to talk to the actor soon or he might lose his job.

When she'd said it was hard to find work in New York, she'd been speaking from personal experience. Melissa had lived in the city for two years, and after she'd had to quit a teaching position she couldn't tolerate she'd used up her savings before finding a part-time library job reading stories to children. She wouldn't have been able to make ends meet if she hadn't been lucky enough to live with a roommate in a rent-controlled apartment. But her roommate had eloped recently and she was in a bind again. Although her neighbor Terry had helped her obtain this Santa's helper position, the job would end at Christmas.

Entering the Santa's Workshop area, Melissa found that it was too late to talk to Santa now. Clarence was already seated and several children were lined up to see him.

"Want to work the end of the line or the beginning?" Arlene asked her, indicating the velvet-rope-lined aisle that led past Santa's chair.

"I'll take the end," Melissa replied. Maybe she'd have time to catch Clarence at the end of the evening. She grabbed a basket of lollipops from behind a counter and took her post. As Arlene kept order at the beginning of the rapidly growing line, Melissa would steer the children out at the end, giving each a Christmas lollipop. Eyeing Clarence with suspicion, Melissa watched him gently lift the first little girl onto his lap and incline his white-haired head. He didn't so much as glance at the waiting adults. So far, it looked like he was behaving himself. Just in case, she intended to observe him closely all evening.

Thinking about her problems with employment again, Melissa tried to shake off a feeling of depression and assume a bright smile for the children. Just because she wouldn't be able to make it home to Pennsylvania for the holidays didn't mean she couldn't spread holiday cheer to others. Still, she wondered what excuse she could give her family. She'd been sick with the flu last year. Did she dare pretend she was sick again? Telling them she didn't have enough money would make her feel too much like a failure. Then Melissa came up with the perfect solution, an excuse that was part truth, part wishful thinking. She'd tell her parents she had to work on Christmas Eve—the truth! —and add she *might* have another job starting immediately the day after Christmas.

"Can I have some candy?" a childish voice interrupted her. The little girl who'd been sitting on Santa's lap was looking at her expectantly.

"Sure, honey." Melissa handed the child a striped lollipop. Then, returning the girl to her waiting mother, she pushed her concerns from her mind. It wasn't all her fault anyway. Economic times were rough nationwide and the tough city of New York had bested stronger people than she. Fluffing out her wings, she determined to think positively—maybe her role as a good fairy would make her able to create some magical miracles for herself.

Several hours and many children later, still keeping an eye on Clarence, Melissa became aware that someone else was watching her. Looking toward the stuffed-toy counter, Melissa noticed an attractive older woman in an expensive-looking red wool coat standing with her boss, Huxley Benton, the promotions director. Sheltered by an almost life-size plush elephant, the two were conversing and staring directly at the pink fairy. Melissa suddenly grew nervous. Was she doing something wrong? Was Hux there to reprimand her? Before she had more time to worry, however, her tall boss and his companion came toward her.

"You're so cute!" exclaimed the lady, smiling warmly and nodding so a few strands of her stylishly cut dark hair fell out of place. "You make a wonderful fairy. Are you an actress when you aren't working at Haldan-Northrop?"

"No. I'm a teacher," Melissa told her, trying to remain unperturbed by the woman's remark about her being cute. This woman was probably trying to be friendly, but Melissa had had enough people tell her she was cute or adorable to

15

last her a lifetime. Being tiny had serious disadvantages as far as she was concerned.

Smiling also, although his eyes remained appraising, Hux stared down at Melissa and folded his long arms across his elegantly tailored chest. "Melissa Ryan, right? I remember the name although I don't recall much else from our interview. You're a teacher? I guess that explains your flair with kids. The little devils act like they actually believe in your character."

"Oh, Hux," the woman remonstrated. "I don't know why you say such mean things about children."

"I'm only joking, Louise. You know I like your grandchildren," Hux told her, then turned back to Melissa. "This is Louise Damon, the mother of an old friend of mine. She's got an idea for some after-hours employment for you."

Before Melissa could say anything, Louise asked, "How would you like to be the tooth fairy? I have a six-year-old granddaughter who would really enjoy it. I'd like to do something special for her since she's had a hard time lately, her parents being divorced and all."

"What do you want me to do?"

"Could you visit our house and leave some money under her pillow tonight, maybe talk to her? It would thrill Gretta to see you in your costume. I can make it worth your while."

"And I'd consider it a personal favor, Melissa," Hux added.

She knew it certainly wouldn't hurt to gain points with her boss, and she might as well get some more use out of the costume she'd had to buy. When Louise offered to pay a substantial fee, Melissa couldn't help but be interested.

"You can take a taxi there and I'll make sure you get home safely," Louise said.

"If you like, I could tell Gretta a story," Melissa offered. "Maybe I can think of something that has to do with teeth."

"That would be lovely," Louise agreed, her dark eyes

16

sparkling. "You'll accept my offer? Can you come after work?"

Melissa noted the scribbled Greenwich Village address Louise gave her. "Okay, but it will be after nine-thirty."

While she worked the last half hour Melissa thought about what she'd do with the unexpected money. The amount wasn't enough to get her back to her small home-town for the holidays, but she could at least send some presents to her family. Smiling to herself as she passed out candy, Melissa thought there was some advantage to living in a large city, after all. Where else would someone be willing to pay so much to have her play the tooth fairy? She couldn't wait to tell her friends Terry and Clarence.

Then, suddenly remembering she was supposed to warn the old actor, she turned to find Santa's chair empty as bells rang throughout the building, signaling the closing of the store. Melissa set off quickly to find Clarence and caught up with him outside the dressing room. Surprisingly, he took what she had to say very well, making Melissa feel like a true good fairy.

As she went to get her belongings she wondered if the rest of the evening would go as well.

It was a few minutes before ten when her taxi stopped in front of the three-story brownstone on a Greenwich Village side street. Even under the dim streetlights her pink costume sparkled where it peeked out below the hem of her well-worn down jacket. Aware of being stared at, she straightened her rhinestone tiara, raised her firm little chin, and regally swept across the sidewalk past a couple of snickering punk rockers. They had a lot of nerve! she thought, eyeing their multicolored hair and mismatched outfits.

Approaching the first-floor entrance of the building as instructed, Melissa took note of the long rectangular mullioned window lined with framed color photographs, most

17

of them portraits of children. Stenciled on the glass, modest gold lettering outlined in black proclaimed this to be the residence of the Raphael Damon Photo Studio. About to ring the bell, she was startled when the door popped open.

"You're here! I was so afraid you might change your mind," Louise Damon said in enthusiastic greeting before stepping back to let Melissa into the entryway. "Come in. Let me take your things."

Melissa dutifully handed over the bag containing her street clothes and shoes before struggling with the jacket. In the dark area to the right she could make out a love seat, two chairs, and a reception desk, but Louise quickly took the garment from her and swept through a door that led to a long inner hallway. Melissa skipped a step to catch up with the taller woman. "Is she asleep?"

"I certainly hope so. Rafe lets Gretta stay up past nine only on special occasions. There's a mirror over there if you want to check your hair or something." Louise pointed to a long oval attached to the wall, then busied herself hanging Melissa's jacket in the closet under the stairway. "By the way, Rafe is my son. He's a well-known photographer," she added proudly.

With a frown of concentration, Melissa carefully reformed the bent wire of her wings, which had been crushed beneath her down jacket. She fluffed her golden curls, but a quick glance at her makeup showed her she didn't need to fool with it. All was intact, including the carefully penciled liner and generous smear of glossy pink lipstick that accentuated her cupid's bow lips.

Then she turned her attention to Louise, noting the elegant way the burgundy and black caftan flowed around the older woman when she moved. "Do you live upstairs?"

"No. My quarters are on this floor in back of the studio and darkroom. I wanted my own space even after my husband died. I value my privacy. Rafe and the children live upstairs. Actually, the attic was done over for Gretta and Hank, so each of us has our privacy when we want it."

"All this space is a real luxury for Manhattan," Melissa said, thinking of the rambling house she grew up in and the contrast it provided to her cramped sixth-floor walk-up.

"We like it." Louise began to climb the first set of stairs and motioned for Melissa to follow. "Shh. I don't want to warn Gretta. I just hope we don't run into my vocal son. I was going to tell Rafe about hiring you after Gretta was tucked in for the night, but he disappeared. Rafe had a long day and yawned all through dinner, so perhaps he's in bed too."

"I'll tiptoe all the way," Melissa promised.

Creeping along silently, she had only a glimpse of the softly lit second-floor space that combined the living and dining rooms.

"I'll wait here," Louise whispered, pressing a large coin into Melissa's small hand. "Gretta's bedroom is on the right at the top of the stairs."

Melissa headed up the carpeted steps and approached the door on tiptoes, then checked the coin she'd leave under Gretta's pillow. The shiny silver dollar winked at her as it reflected the soft stairway light. A bubble of excited laughter caught in her throat as she pictured the sleepy little girl's pleasure when Gretta wakened to hear a story told by her very own tooth fairy.

Turning the knob slowly, Melissa winced when it clicked, then gritted her teeth when the door creaked open. She peered into the dark room, willing her eyes to adjust. A white-canopied bed dimly glowed with ghostly intensity against its shadowed surroundings. When she noted the form curled in it, Melissa was assured the little girl was unaware of her presence.

Clutching the silver dollar, she half-blindly maneuvered around the bed, biting her lip when her floating tulle skirt caught on the canopy post. Carefully, she removed the

19

material, squinting hard at the lump under the covers as it moved, turned, and finally settled down with a muffled sigh. Barely able to make out the shape, Melissa frowned. The form seemed large for a toothless six-year-old. Gretta must be big for her age.

Stifling an excited giggle, she moved forward, ears attuned to the soft sounds issuing from beneath the covers as well as to the slightly irregular beat of her own heart. Was Gretta dreaming? she wondered. Very carefully, she reached out and leaned over the still form to slip her closed fist under the pillow, there to relinquish her precious treasure and search for the tooth. It was at that moment that the lump in the bed stirred once more, capturing Melissa's delicate form with a solid, warm grip.

"Mmm, let me thank you properly for rescuing me," a low, sleepy voice appreciatively crooned a hairsbreadth from her lips. Strong arms tightened and her tiny feet flipped up from the floor, throwing her hard against a very male chest.

"Oh!" Melissa's cry of surprise was muffled by a warm, seductive mouth, and her thoughts became muddled by the unexpected yet tingling embrace. It happened so fast she didn't think to resist at first.

Strong hands pulled her closer, making the flesh of her arms and back throb. Insistent lips caressed her own until they quivered and parted at the silent demand. Breathing in the heady scent of spice, Melissa was magically enticed by the seductive assault.

Then, gasping for air, she came out of her enchanted trance, suddenly horrified that she was kissing a complete stranger and enjoying it. What in the world had come over her? Her body tingled naughtily everywhere it touched his. When she struggled to free herself, flailing her arms and legs in protest, the tingling sensation intensified. She struggled more vigorously and managed to pull her lips free. Her rhinestone tiara dropped off her head and her fist came in contact with a solid object, then something flew to the floor with a loud crash.

"What the—" a deep voice growled beneath her.

"Please, let go of me!" she gasped from her perch atop him.

And then the door burst open and light flooded the room. Inanely, Melissa stared at her rhinestone tiara, which had fallen on a decidedly masculine brow.

"Daddy!" two young voices exclaimed.

"What happened?" Louise shouted, gasping as she reached the top of the stairs. "Oh, good heavens!"

Five pairs of eyes widened as the tableau froze for one interminable moment. Rafe Damon was the first to find his voice. "Who are you?" he demanded of the lovely creature who assaulted his senses.

Her face turned the same becoming shade of pink as her dress. "I'm, uhh—"

"The tooth fairy!" Gretta yelled, running to the bed. "Gran said she'd come! Let go of her, Daddy! You're crushing her wings!"

The little girl hopped onto the bed and frowned at her father, who still cradled the human bundle in his arms. With a guilty start, Rafe pushed the tooth fairy away from his throbbing body and sat straight up. He scowled as the tiara flipped off his head, bounced off his chest, and landed on the bed as the golden-haired young woman slipped to the floor with a jarring thunk.

"Sorry," he croaked, almost strangling on the word as he realized what had just transpired. One minute he'd been dreaming, the next hotly embracing a strange young woman.

"What are you doing in Gretta's bed?" Louise asked faintly, looking from Rafe to Melissa, then back to Rafe.

Rafe rose quickly. He pulled his robe tighter, cinching the belt around his waist. "Gretta was afraid she'd have another nightmare, so I said I'd stay with her until she fell asleep." He raked his fingers through his dark hair. "But I guess I fell asleep instead. I was the one who had a nightmare and thought she . . . uh, rescued me," he muttered a little sheepishly.

"Gretta was in my room," Hank announced. "We were playing video games with my computer."

"Hank! You weren't supposed to tell!" Gretta shouted at her older brother, getting to her pajama-covered feet and jumping up and down in the middle of her bed.

Rafe glanced down at the pink confection and into her cornflower-blue eyes. At his blatant perusal, she frowned and blinked fiercely, but didn't look away.

"I believe this is yours."

Rescuing the tiara from the threat of being trampled under his daughter's feet, Rafe held it out. The lovely creature took the crown and fixed it in her soft curls. When her wavering smile dimpled her cheek, he felt an unwanted flush of heat sear him. Good Lord, what was wrong with him? She had to be in her early twenties, certainly too young for a man with two kids.

"Daddy, stop hogging my tooth fairy!" Gretta demanded. "I wanna play with her."

Melissa tore her gaze away from the man's dark eyes with heavy lids—sexy bedroom eyes, she thought uneasily—and turned to the girl, who was dressed in dark green one-piece pajamas. She was still standing in the middle of the canopied bed, her arms crossed over her chest. With her waist-length dark hair and long bangs crowding her puckered brows, she looked like an angry little elf.

"All right, sweetheart." Rafe leaned over and kissed his daughter, then ruffled her bangs. "We'll leave you and the tooth fairy alone."

"Good."

"I never had a tooth fairy," Hank grumbled disgustedly as he was ushered out the door. "I had a deprived childhood."

Hiding her smile behind her hand, Melissa guessed the boy, who was a smaller version of his father, must be all of eleven or twelve. Obviously, he was resenting the attention his little sister was getting.

"Are you a *real* tooth fairy?" Gretta asked in an excited whisper once the room was cleared.

Melissa's lips twitched. "What do you think?"

Gretta smiled broadly, showing off her newest space where she'd lost the tooth. "I think we should pretend." She used the bed as a trampoline once more. "You can be my very own tooth fairy for tonight. What can you do besides leave money under my pillow?"

"I can tell you a story if you get ready to go to sleep."

Gretta trampolined down to her knees and scrambled under her covers. "About a fairy princess?"

"About a dragon!" Melissa said fiercely, inspired by the bedroom walls, which were painted like scenery in the pages of a storybook. "One who lost a tooth."

"Yea! Was it a big dragon?"

"A big, cranky dragon who hated any kind of changes. When he lost his tooth, he wanted it back, no matter what."

Melissa went on to tell Gretta about how unreasonable the dragon was and the tricks he played on the villagers until he found his tooth. Of course she made the heroine a beautiful little girl with dark hair and dark eyes who charmed the dragon so nicely that he gave her his tooth as a vase for her flowers.

"Was the little girl's name Gretta?"

"I don't know. The dragon didn't tell me her name," Melissa said, tucking the blanket under Gretta's chin. "Now it's time for you to get some sleep."

"But I'm not sleepy. Besides, you can't go yet. Daddy has to take our picture first, or else how am I gonna prove you were here when I tell my friends 'bout you?"

Noting the stubborn tilt to her chin, Melissa quickly acquiesced. Gretta raced out of the room to inform her father they were going down to the studio to have pictures taken. Seemingly over any embarrassment he might have felt at their accidental embrace, Rafe readily gave in to his daughter's request. Louise came along to watch, but Hank refused to be any part of the project. He insisted he had some homework he'd forgotten about earlier, but Melissa could tell it was an excuse.

While Rafe Damon snapped pictures of her and Gretta, Melissa studied him surreptitiously, keeping her manner aloof. His dark bedroom eyes, which seemed to follow her every movement and analyze her every expression, certainly went with his attire. His black robe with a rolled white collar over white-on-white pin-striped pajama bottoms enhanced his dark good looks—olive skin, black hair with a natural wave, and more dark hair sprinkled over the expanse of chest peeking through the robe's V neck. And his body was pretty sexy, even if it was only five-seven or so. Actually, his reasonable height was appealing to a woman who often wore three-inch heels to give herself credibility.

He was attractive, Melissa reluctantly admitted, trying not to let his bold stare get to her. It unsettled her, made her feel as though he'd like to do more than take her in his arms and kiss her again—exactly the type of man she made a point to avoid.

"That's it," Rafe finally said, to Melissa's relief. He turned off the photofloods and, looking at Gretta, added, "Bed for you, young lady."

"Do I gotta?"

"Yes, you gotta!" But the fierce scowl he aimed at his daughter was softened by a crooked smile that sent gooseflesh crawling all over Melissa's body. "Now, scoot."

Gretta held up her arms and Rafe stooped so she could give him a big hug and kiss. "G'night, Daddy." Then she went scampering away with her grandmother following.

"I'll see that she gets tucked in," Louise said. "And, Melissa, thank you for coming. You were wonderful and Gretta was as thrilled as I'd hoped." The older woman slipped the agreed amount of money into the tooth fairy's hand and whispered, "Sorry about the mix-up."

"I enjoyed it," Melissa admitted, then, because she didn't want Louise—or Rafe, whose eyes now bored into her back —to think she meant the unexpected embrace, she quickly added, "I mean playing the tooth fairy for Gretta." But Louise was already gone. At the amused male chuckle behind her, Melissa realized she was once more alone with the photographer, a situation not to her liking. She cleared her throat uneasily. "I'll just get my things."

As she started toward the closet, Rafe's words stopped her cold. "Don't rush off. It will take me only a minute to get out of my pajamas."

Shocked at his blatant suggestion, Melissa whirled around. "Don't you dare take them off!"

His lips quivered and his eyes lit as he insisted, "I can't see you home dressed like this. I might get arrested."

What a blunder! Flushing, she realized Louise must have asked Rafe to see her home safely while Melissa told Gretta the dragon story. And yet, she thought suspiciously, wasn't the photographer's expression speculative, sort of like a dragon contemplating its next tasty morsel?

"Don't worry about it." Melissa backed up nervously. No man had ever looked at her in quite that way before, and she wasn't sure she liked it. "You don't have to take me home."

"Of course I do if I want to make sure you get there safely," he said, advancing on her. "This city is dangerous at night."

Rafe was the one who looked dangerous, Melissa thought, noting his slow smile and bemused expression, the invitation in his dark eyes. She'd probably be safer going home alone.

"How are you planning to get home anyway? By flying?"

His bedroom eyes roamed over her wings as Rafe moved closer, practically forcing Melissa to back into the closet. "You're such a cute little fairy. Dainty wings, dainty feet, dainty mouth . . ."

His face only inches away, Melissa was sure he was going to kiss her. Whirling around, she found her jacket and bag and pushed by him. "I've got to get going." She tried to keep her voice steady, unlike the unexpected thundering of her heart. She couldn't believe the man had the nerve to try to make a pass at her! If he weren't a friend of her boss, she'd tell Rafe Damon a thing or two.

Before she could get her jacket on, he reached out and touched the wire and net wings. "How is this costume put together anyway? Are the wings attached or do they come off first?"

That did it. Did Rafe Damon think his blatant come-on was sexy or something? "Stuff it, Mr. Damon. I'm leaving *now.*"

Struggling into her jacket, she stormed out of the building, ignoring his earnest, "Melissa, wait a minute, please!"

Melissa couldn't believe the man had made her lose her temper so quickly. She'd been raised to think the best of people, to stay out of arguments, and not to say anything if it weren't something nice. She'd learned her parents' philosophy so well they had called her their "little angel," although her best friend had given her the disgusting nickname of "Goody Two-Shoes."

Already feeling guilty and highly resentful that Rafe Damon had so easily made her cross her principles, Melissa huffed her way over to Christopher Street, where she flagged down a taxi she really couldn't afford.

CHAPTER TWO

Catching the eight-by-ten prints as they fell from the rotating drum of the dryer, Rafe carefully laid the black and white glossies of Gretta and her tooth fairy on the counter. He examined them closely.

His daughter was a real imp, he thought proudly, smiling at her various expressions. She'd really hammed it up, alternately smiling, frowning, and sticking out her tongue. In contrast, the tooth fairy was mostly aloof in front of the camera, seeming to have her mind on other things. But there was one shot in which she'd looked straight into the lens, and the expression in her eyes made his blood sizzle.

Whew!

Melissa Ryan. Louise had told him that was the tooth fairy's real name. Staring down at the photo in his hand, Rafe cursed softly as he vainly tried to control his masculine reaction to her fragile, innocent beauty. The other night he'd been unable to stop himself from teasing her unmercifully until she'd lost her temper. Then, when she'd run out onto the street, he'd felt guilty.

To be truthful, what he'd really wanted to do was take Melissa in his arms to kiss her again.

Rafe hit the counter with the flat of his hand. That was the problem! He wanted to kiss her even now, but, dammit, she was too young for him. Yet he couldn't help being attracted to the golden-haired, blue-eyed doll who'd accidentally landed in bed with him. For the past two nights he'd had a rough time sleeping; he couldn't eradicate her magical image from his mind.

Rafe had never thought of himself as one of those men who tried to recapture his youth by courting some pretty young thing. But wasn't that precisely what his mind—not to mention his body—was telling him to do? How ridiculous. He was a thirty-two-year-old man lusting after a younger woman who was probably right out of college. How old could Melissa be? Twenty-two? Ten years made a big difference, especially when two kids were involved.

Still, Rafe regretted scaring Melissa away as he had. His actions had been uncharacteristic. He'd probably come on to her so strong because he'd had a hard day and one drink too many to relax. That or frustration must be warping his hormones. Maybe he ought to start visiting singles bars to find a woman his own age. Rafe tried not to cringe in distaste. He'd tried that scene a few times after he'd gotten over the betrayal of his divorce, but while he'd come away from the short-lived encounters physically gratified, he'd been left emotionally empty.

When friends had fixed him up on blind dates, he hadn't been any happier. Besides, not many women seemed to be in the market for a ready-made family—at least not the women he'd met.

Why couldn't he meet a mature, charming, affectionate woman who had a good sense of humor and liked children? Rafe wondered. Was that so much to ask? Although they weren't part of his requirements, it wouldn't hurt if she had golden hair and blue eyes and was small enough to look up at him . . .

A bang at the door brought him out of his reverie. "What's up?" he shouted, thinking it was Louise.

"It's me. Hux. You developing?"

Guiltily, Rafe gathered the photos into a neat pile and turned them upside down on the counter. "I'm finished. Come on in."

"Hey, you old son-of-a-gun," Hux greeted him with enthusiasm, clapping him on the back. "Long time, no see!"

"Don't worry, you'll see me plenty at Haldan-Northrop tomorrow," Rafe said, referring to the photo layout of Santa's Workshop he'd been contracted to do.

"Yeah, but what's life coming to when you can't find time to make arrangements with me personally? Now you send Louise to do your dirty work."

"I thought you liked Louise."

"Hey, pal, I love your mother. I have since you brought me home for Christmas vacation the year my parents were in Switzerland," Hux said, referring to their college days.

"With the holidays coming up, I've got too many bookings to attend to all the preliminary work."

"Ah, success." Hux perched his lean, well-tanned body on a stool next to Rafe's work counter and stretched out his long legs. "Does anything smell sweeter?"

"You tell me."

"How about a woman's perfume? That's why I stopped by. I want you to come to Limelight with me tonight. The ladies who frequent the place are nothing short of spectacular."

"Hux, don't you think a nightclub in a former church seems a little . . . tacky?"

"Nah, not when it's done in good taste, which it is. All the beautiful people agree."

And he was one of them. With a decent amount of money, a classy style, and fair good looks, Huxley Benton was considered quite a catch. A perennial bachelor, he planned to stay that way, and Rafe had no doubts that he would. His friend enjoyed the single life to the fullest, and he couldn't imagine Hux tied down to one woman or to kids, whom the pseudocynic professed to hate.

"I'm going to pass on this one," Rafe told him firmly. "I need my beauty rest so I can do a great job for you tomorrow."

"Okay, if that's the way you want— Hey, what's this?" Hux had elbowed the short stack of photos, then had lifted one to look at it. His eyes lit with recognition and he whistled. "Wow. That sugarplum fairy is some doll, huh? Do I know how to pick them or what?"

Rafe bristled at his friend's wolfish tone and grabbed the photo out of Hux's hand. It was the one with *the* expression.

Hux merely picked up another of the prints and inspected it more closely. "You know, the kid's got something."

"Forget it. She's too young for you."

Hux looked puzzled, then shrugged. "Hey, you know I don't mix business with pleasure. I'm interested professionally. I want you to do some test shots for me. Maybe I could use her at the store in some future promotions."

Rafe had been prepared to deal with Melissa Ryan at Santa's Workshop for the photo layout, but working with her alone? That's all he needed.

"Listen, Hux, you'd better get someone else. I've already got so many appointments booked—"

"Rafe, you owe me one. Remember the Baby Bountiful ads I threw your way last month? Do me this favor and we're square."

With a deep sigh, knowing his tenacious friend wouldn't give up until he did, Rafe agreed, smiling to himself as he remembered Melissa's charms. "All right. I know when to say uncle."

Hux took the print back out of Rafe's hand and smiled wolfishly, showing perfect white teeth as he studied it. "Look at that expression! This little pink sugarplum fairy's got something all right. And I want you to get it for me." He winked one green eye. "In photographs, that is."

Rafe looked forward to seeing Melissa Ryan in spite of his reservations. When he got her alone in his studio—well, a little flirtation couldn't hurt anything, could it?

"How come you're not excited about this photo session?" Arlene asked Melissa as they changed into their costumes. "Our picture might be in *The New York Times!*"

"Maybe I'm coming down with the flu," Melissa told the black woman, sniffling for effect as she slid her feet into pink satin slippers.

" 'Tis the season."

Actually, she was in a funky mood this morning, but it had nothing to do with her health. She'd spent another restless night wondering how long it would be before she'd get to sleep. What in the world was wrong with her?

"I'm ready to go down to the Workshop. Are you coming?" she asked Arlene.

"You kidding? Does this face look like it's ready? If I'm gonna be in pictures, I gotta prepare, honey."

Melissa shook her head at Arlene's dramatics as she left the women's dressing room.

"Ho-ho-ho!" The booming voice was followed by a jolly red-clothed body. "If it isn't my favorite sugarplum fairy. And what do you want for Christmas, little one?"

"Why, Santa!" Melissa looked up past the white beard to Clarence's rosy cheeks and nose. She hoped the color was merely makeup. "Umm, how about . . . financial stability and romance?"

"Granted!" he said in character, then switched to his real self. "I'd do anything I could to make your wishes come true, Melissa. It's not often someone comes to the aid of an old reprobate."

"Oh, Clarence, I didn't do anything but give you some advice."

"That in itself is precious, my dear girl. I need this job desperately, and you convinced the others to give me a second chance before ratting on me. Terry told me," he said, referring to Melissa's neighbor and their mutual friend who played the green elf. "You're a ray of sunshine in a cold, cruel city. A jewel amidst paste. A rose among the thorns." Bowing sharply from the waist, he took her hand and kissed it, reminding Melissa of Terry's claim that Clarence fancied himself a leading man. "Consider me in your debt."

Embarrassed by his effusive thanks, Melissa blushed. Had a few sincere words meant so much to the man? She'd always thought Clarence's antics were a humorous facade, anyway—a bid for attention from a lonely old man—but she'd never taken him seriously.

"Don't be silly. A simple thank you will do."

"Hardly, my girl, hardly. Hmm. You yearn for financial stability? With your looks, you should be able to get ads, perhaps commercials."

"I'm not a model or an actress. I'm a teacher."

"Don't worry. I can help you find an agent who won't hold that against you."

"An agent? Where?" asked Terry, catching up to them just as they stepped on the escalator that would take them down to Santa's Workshop. He leaned over and used a loud stage whisper to inform Melissa, "No self-respecting agent would let Clarence in his office these days."

"Bah humbug!"

Melissa snorted at Clarence's out-of-character line and at the resulting bickering. Those two were always picking on each other, but she wasn't worried that the verbal battle would erupt into a physical one. She knew Terry and Clarence had been good friends for a couple of years, ever since they were extras in a fast-food-chain commercial.

Melissa realized she felt comfortable with these two men because their good-natured banter reminded her of Andy and Luke. A wave of nostalgia hit her when she thought that this would be the second Christmas in a row she wouldn't be able to spend with her two younger brothers. And who knew where Andy would be next year after he graduated from college? There weren't many jobs for industrial engineers in Pennsylvania these days. Her good mood plunged downward with the descent of the escalator.

But Melissa didn't have time to feel sad. A minute later she stepped off the escalator and into Haldan-Northrop's magical Christmas kingdom.

Santa's Workshop was aglow with light even though it was early morning. Toys were creatively displayed in elegant groupings around giant papier-mâché representations. There was the doll house with its new and antique dolls, the polar bear with its stuffed toys, the locomotive with its train sets, and the rocking horse with its smaller counterparts.

A few children tugged mothers around the incredible displays, but Melissa knew they were models for the advertisement; it would be hours before the store opened. Lights and reflectors were already in place for the photo layout that would take most of the day. Kids who wanted to see Santa Claus would have to wait until late that evening.

As she passed the enchanted castle set on a mountain, Melissa stopped as she always did to admire the massive display. There were delightful animated people and creatures in windows, on balconies, and along the mountain road. Three miniature brass trains chugged through the tunnels on various levels. Each time she viewed the display Melissa picked out new and charming details.

Inspecting one of the castle's turrets closely, she noticed a tiny blond princess dressed in pink and white who stood near a dark prince. When the princess glanced up, the prince's eyebrows lifted and then her eyes batted furiously. She looked down and he took a half step toward her, but quickly stepped back when she glanced up again. The flirtatious, animated scenario was so delightful, Melissa laughed.

"Hey, Melissa, come on," Terry whispered. "The photographer's anxious to get started."

Melissa regretfully pulled herself away from the enchanted castle and joined Terry and the others, who were gathered in a group. There was an expectant hush as they waited for their instructions, and Melissa asked Clarence to let her get in front of her so she could see. When she did her jaw went slack. Why hadn't she guessed the identity of the photographer who would do the layout?

There, a few feet away, stood Rafe Damon, staring at her. Then he quickly looked away. Why? Because he was ashamed of the way he'd treated her the night before? If not, he *should* be, Melissa thought belligerently, remembering how forward he'd been. She was sure Rafe knew how uncomfortable he'd made her feel, but that hadn't stopped him from trying to take advantage of her.

Then he turned to say something to his assistant, a pretty young woman in jeans and a voluminous sweater. Was she his girlfriend? Her eyes strayed to the other woman's left hand, which was pointing to a light. Melissa smiled when a diamond sparkled from her ring finger, then she clenched her jaw in disgust. What did she care if the woman was married or not?

"We're set up and ready to begin," Rafe said succinctly. "Although the children are models, they're still kids at heart. I'd like them to act as naturally as possible. I don't want to pose shots unless it's absolutely necessary, so act like you would normally with the kids, only do it better. I'm going to move around while I shoot. Please try to pretend I don't exist," he ordered. "I'll tell you if I want something special. Okay, let's get to work."

Melissa tried to resent his imperious tone, but she couldn't, no more than she could stop herself from admiring the way Rafe filled out his black jeans and turtleneck, clothes that enhanced his dark good looks. Her eyes strayed to him again and again as she worked, until Melissa grew increasingly irritated with herself, especially when he caught her at it. She blinked and looked down at her basket of lollipops.

Why couldn't she forget those bedroom eyes?

"Boy, I wish I could afford equipment like his," the teddy bear grumbled softly. Melissa offered a piece of candy to the child leaving Santa, then turned to the Santa's Workshop photographer.

"Don't worry, someday you'll be able to afford the kind of equipment you really want. Remember, you're just starting in your career," Melissa said, hoping to cheer him. "He's been in the business for years. You're neither as experienced nor as old as Rafe Damon."

What was that supposed to mean? Rafe wondered, overhearing her comment while taking a shot of her and the teddy bear in the foreground with Santa and one of the kids in the background. He was annoyed that Melissa so blatantly reminded him of the difference in their ages. He wasn't that old. Had she guessed he was interested in her? Was she telling the others? Melissa laughed and the tinkling sound played havoc with Rafe's pulse. Was she laughing at him too?

"Excuse me for interrupting your personal conversation, Melissa, but I need your complete cooperation during this photo session," Rafe told her with mock innocence. "Do you think you could get creative for me? I know, you could flutter your wings!"

Melissa seemed startled and her cornflower-blue eyes widened, making Rafe ashamed of himself for teasing her. Her cupid's bow mouth opened as if to contradict him, but she shut it with a snap, tossed her golden tresses, and turned to one of the children, nearly shoving her wings in his face. Rafe stifled the urge to laugh. It served him right. What an adorable fairy she was!

All through the shoot Rafe kept reminding himself that she was too young to pursue seriously, but he lost the mental game he played. When noon approached he wondered how he'd managed to work at all. Every time he looked up, the magical vision in pink seemed to block his view. Or was it that his eyes were drawn to her wherever she might be? Damn! He just hoped he'd gotten some decent photos.

Shaking his head in disgust, Rafe looked around for his assistant, Pam, but once more his eyes strayed elsewhere. There, on the other side of Santa's Workshop, Melissa was laughing with the green elf. Was that bozo her boyfriend?

"Lunchtime, everyone!" he shouted. "Employees, be back in forty-five minutes. Kids are through for the day."

Then Rafe stalked the pink fairy and green elf, thinking this was as good a time as any to tell Melissa about the test shots Hux wanted.

"The guy's pretty creative," Terry was saying to Melissa. "I heard him tell his assistant he was going to set us up on the individual displays after lunch. You know, get some fun shots of Santa's helpers playing with the toys. I can see why he's successful. Rafe Damon's a real dynamo."

"He can be overbearing, all right."

"Well, maybe he has a touch of a Napoleon complex. Small men sometimes do."

Melissa laughed up at her freckle-faced friend. "You should talk. You've got to be two inches shorter than he is."

"The packaging may be similar, but the difference is in the personality."

"I'm sure he's got a softer side to him," Melissa insisted, not knowing why she should say anything nice about the pushy photographer.

"Hmm, defending him, are you? You wouldn't have a thing for a certain man with dark hair, dark eyes, and a Napoleon complex, would you?"

"No!"

"Excuse me, but I've got to talk to Melissa for a minute." Rafe's voice came from behind her, interrupting the rest of her protest. "Alone."

Melissa whirled around angrily. "I just heard you tell

36

everyone it was time for lunch, so don't you dare intimate I was goofing off again."

"I wasn't about to."

"Excuse me," Terry said, backing off in spite of the plea Melissa knew he recognized in her eyes. He winked at her mischievously. "I told Clarence I'd have lunch with him and he's an impatient man when it comes to food."

"What do you want, Rafe?" Melissa demanded impatiently, crossing her arms.

"How about coming to my studio tomorrow, so I can take some test shots of you?"

"I have no interest in posing for your photographs."

"What do you call what you've been doing this morning?"

"My job. For Haldan-Northrop."

"The test shots are *for* Haldan-Northrop. More specifically for Huxley Benton. He asked me to take them as a personal favor."

Sure he did, Melissa thought, suspicious of Rafe's motives. She knew the two men were good friends and that Hux had a reputation as a playboy. Undoubtedly, both men were cut from the same cloth. So Rafe wanted to get her alone, did he? To repeat—or complete—the performance begun in Gretta's bed? Having lived in New York for nearly two years, she wasn't so naive that she couldn't figure it out.

"Well?" Rafe asked, leaning over Melissa and resting his hand on the display behind her. "How about it?"

Inching away from his encroaching body, she said, "Next you'll tell me Louise and the kids will be there to watch."

"I don't know about Louise. She's in and out, depending on what errands she has to run. The kids will be in school."

"How convenient." Melissa was not about to set herself up to be alone with him; what if he wanted pictures of her in the nude or something? "But I won't be there, either."

"What's the matter, Melissa?" Rafe raised a dark brow

and his lips twitched. "Don't you trust yourself to be alone with me after the way you kissed me?"

"After the way *I*—why you—"

"It's nothing to be ashamed of." He inclined his head and lowered his voice. "I've been told I'm a pretty good kisser." Melissa began sputtering again, until he added, "But then, so are you. Do you sprinkle fairy dust over every man you meet?"

Wide-eyed, Melissa stared at the attractive photographer as if he were the one spreading around fairy dust. When Rafe ran his fingers over one of her wings, she shivered as if he were touching her body. When he leaned closer she thought he would kiss her again, and she couldn't move away to save herself.

Suddenly, Huxley Benton's voice broke the spell and Melissa took a relieved breath when Rafe straightened and moved away.

"There you are, Rafe. Are you two discussing the test shots?"

"There's nothing to discuss. Melissa's not interested."

Hux's handsome face frowned down at her. "Melissa, why not? I might be able to use you for other promotions in the future."

"I . . . well . . ."

"Really. Kids take to you. I've got an idea I've been working on, and you might be the perfect person for the job."

Her financial uncertainty rising in her mind, Melissa let him sway her, albeit reluctantly. More than ever, she was wary of the playboy photographer. "All right. I'll do it."

"Be at my place at one."

"Fine." She avoided Rafe's eyes. "Now can I go to lunch?"

Hurrying to the employee cafeteria, Melissa thought about Rafe. At least the test shots were legitimate, though she couldn't say the same for his behavior. Remembering how he'd so blatantly come on to her, she repressed the slight thrill that ran through her and concentrated on the fact that she'd always disliked pushy men.

CHAPTER THREE

Melissa wished she could stop being so nervous. She hoped she had no real reason to be. On the short subway ride to the Village, she'd kept telling herself to relax, the photography session would be strictly professional. Surely Rafe Damon wouldn't take advantage of a work situation, would he? Besides, despite his pointed remarks and sly glances, she'd decided to give the photographer the benefit of the doubt. Perhaps she'd made a rash judgment based on past negative experiences.

Melissa knew she tended to be defensive about men. She'd never liked it when an escort tried to be overprotective, equating her petite size with helplessness. Nor did she like it when big-city types approached her with confident conceit, trying to bowl her over with charm, undoubtedly believing they could seduce her into a fast-paced affair or a one-night stand. Why couldn't men appreciate old-fashioned courtship? What was wrong with allowing casual dating to mature to a more serious relationship, which, in turn, might develop into permanent commitment?

She sighed. Surely there were men around somewhere who would appreciate her values and she'd find one to her liking eventually. Too bad Rafe Damon was so darn attractive. Melissa was sure he didn't fall into the acceptable category.

Switching her dress bag to her other hand, she approached the entrance to Rafe's studio. A thrill of trepidation ran through her as she gazed up at the photographs in the window. What if he gave her a difficult time today? Could she manage to keep him at arm's length and still get through the session? Hux had hinted she might be able to earn extra money if he liked the test shots. She'd have to use that incentive to give herself courage. Straightening her tense shoulders, Melissa mounted the steps and rang the bell.

Rafe opened the door himself, his dark brown eyes sweeping over her appreciatively, his full lips spreading into a charming grin. "Hello, Melissa," he said, holding the door open to let her in. "You're right on time. I've got the studio all set up."

Gliding by carefully in order to avoid touching him, Melissa caught a whiff of spicy masculine cologne as she went to the hall closet to hang up her coat and the garment bag with her costume in it. Her heart was pounding a little faster than normal and she jumped when she turned and nearly bumped into him.

"Oh! You startled me."

"Don't worry. I won't try to back you into the closet. I thought we'd try something different today."

"I certainly hope so!"

Rafe cleared his throat. He looked like he was trying to keep from laughing. She hoped she hadn't given him more ideas; he seemed to have enough of his own.

"The studio's that way. Want to trip lightly on in and take the seat in front of the camera?"

"That's what I'm here for, isn't it?" she asked irritably, walking away with dignified steps.

He'd placed a high stool amid all the lighting equipment. Because her legs were too short to hook her heels over the bottom rung, Melissa made herself comfortable by crossing her ankles and leaning against the chair's high back. Looking around the space, she didn't see Rafe's assistant anywhere, but perhaps the young woman didn't work with him every day. Obviously, they were going to be alone.

"You pout well," he said, looking at her through the Hasselblad camera.

"I'm not pouting."

"Well, whatever you're doing, you're very photogenic. You look as cute as an angry sugar cookie."

"Let's leave out the cute remarks, okay?"

"What's wrong with cute? You may as well use any qualities others see in you to your personal advantage. All professional models do."

"I'm not a professional model."

"You could be for some Haldan-Northrop promotions if Hux likes these shots. I'm sure he'll want you to appear sweet and wholesome."

Knowing he was right, Melissa conceded, "All right. I'll try my best to pose as you want. I like to think there are aspects to my personality that are more positive than cute, that's all."

"Well, maybe we can explore those today too." His tone was soft and seductive. Gazing into his intense, hooded eyes, she could imagine them heated with desire. "Exploring can be very exciting."

Was he suggesting something questionable? Melissa glared at him fiercely. "What do you mean by that remark?"

"I mean we can try different expressions, different shots if you like. You'll have to tell me a little about yourself." Rafe's eyes raked her intently. "Maybe I'll get some ideas for poses that will reveal the real you."

"What would you like to know?" she asked suspiciously, wondering if this was where he got personal.

"Ah, ha! Your eyes are lighting up with interest." He peered into the camera. "Now turn a little to the left. That's good." The shutter clicked. "Try smiling dreamily.

42

Tilt your chin up. Good. How long have you been one of Santa's helpers? Do you play the role every year?"

That was it? Having thought he was about to delve into her love life or something, Melissa heaved a sigh of relief and said, "This is my first time."

"How did you get the job?"

"I found out about it through a friend and applied."

"Is helping Santa your usual kind of work?"

"Of course. I'm a holiday specialist. I plan to dress up as an Easter egg with legs in the spring." Melissa smirked. Unused to being sarcastic, she found it hard to carry off with a straight face.

"I suppose you'll be a firecracker by summer."

"Probably."

Watching the photographer adjust some lights on metal stands, Melissa admired the way the beige cableknit sweater he wore with neat brown pants hugged his compact form. Thinking about clothing made her remember to ask him about her costume.

"I didn't know whether or not you wanted to photograph me in my costume, so I brought it. I can take these things off if you want." She regretted the words as soon as they were out of her mouth.

Continuing to work with the lights, Rafe had a wicked gleam in his eye. "Feel free to take off any clothes you want to."

Melissa had known this was going to happen! "If you think I'm going to take off my—"

"Since these are only test shots, it doesn't matter what you wear." He took a good look at her and shrugged. "What you've got on is fine."

Even though she was relieved he didn't expect her to undress, Melissa wished he appreciated the trouble she'd gone to with her appearance this morning. Did he think she was wearing any old outfit? She'd searched through her closet at least three times before settling on a pale blue

sweater and a full cotton skirt worn over some lacy, berib-
boned antique petticoats. Teaming the garments with
high-heeled lace-up boots, Melissa had thought she looked
quite romantic. But perhaps Rafe preferred a more sophisticated look for a woman. She clenched her jaw. She
shouldn't even wonder what Rafe would like in a woman.
What did she care?

"So, you're a sugarplum fairy. I thought you were into
teeth."

"Santa Claus wouldn't have a tooth fairy for a helper,
would he?" Melissa asked primly, glad he'd returned to a
safe topic.

"No, I suppose not. Tilt your chin down. Why did you
pick New York for your dramatic debut? Does your family
live here or have you been going to school?"

How old did he think she was? "I haven't been in school
for a long time—at least, not as a student." At his questioning look, she explained. "I was only joking about being a
holiday specialist. I'm a teacher. Last year I taught a sixth-
grade class in the public school system."

"Really? You must have graduated a couple of years ago
then. I wouldn't call that such a long time."

Rafe examined the lens of the camera. His casual attitude
made Melissa think he didn't believe her.

"I graduated from college six years ago," she insisted,
wondering why she felt compelled to make him believe
what she said. "Before I came to New York, I taught second
grade for four years in a small town near Williamsport,
Pennsylvania. Since I didn't have much tenure, I was laid
off when enrollment went down. That's when I came to
New York to get a job."

"Hmm."

Melissa crossed her legs and raised her chin slightly. "I'm
twenty-eight years old, you know."

He stared at her. "Oh, come on."

"Do you want to see my driver's license?"

44

"Twenty-eight? Seriously?" Rafe's scoffing expression changed. Suddenly, he seemed really interested in whatever she had to say. "Why aren't you teaching now? Did you give it all up for the toy department?"

"No. The job didn't work out." Melissa wasn't about to explain that she'd felt overwhelmed by kids who were larger than she was and intimidated by some of their hardened, inner-city personalities. "Now I have a part-time job with the library system in the reading enrichment program. I tell small children stories to get them interested in reading. I've also applied to some private schools for teaching positions."

Rafe moved to her side and put his hands on her shoulders. "Keep them straight." Then he slipped his hands around her waist. "But turn your lower body this way." Melissa was trying to catch her breath from the effects of his warm fingers when he asked, "So if you're really a twenty-eight-year-old teacher, where did this crazy sugarplum fairy job come from?"

"Until I get an appropriate full-time position, I pick up part-time work in addition to the reading program."

"Really?" Rafe cupped her face and tilted it toward the light. "This pose should be flattering."

Their noses were scant inches apart. Was he thinking about making a pass? Feeling uncomfortable and defensive, Melissa pulled back. Talking about her job problems had brought up bad memories. Now he was making her edgy with his physical manipulations.

"Do you have to stand so close?"

"I'm just trying to do my job. Is your hair color natural?"

"Do you interrogate all your subjects like this?"

"Interrogate? No, I always try to establish rapport. With the really small ones, I have to make faces or do other silly things to get them interested."

"That sounds weird."

"It isn't weird. They like it."

45

"What kind of strange small women do you photograph?"

"Women?" Rafe had a puzzled look on his face.

"Your models," she insisted.

"I don't usually photograph women. I specialize in children."

"Really?"

"Yeah." Rafe's questioning frown turned into an expression of amused enlightenment as he finally caught the drift of her meaning. A wide grin split his face. "Hey, what kind of work do you think I do? Sorry to disappoint you, but the only nudes I do are babies on bearskin rugs. Want to see my portfolio?"

A giggle started low in her throat. Then Rafe snorted. Soon they were both laughing uproariously.

Rafe shook his head at Melissa's assumption. He could hardly believe she'd thought he was a girlie magazine photographer. Was that why she'd been so cool with him? Because she'd disapproved? No doubt she had assumed he'd wanted her to take off her clothes, Rafe thought, remembering he'd told her to feel free . . . He hadn't been able to stop himself from teasing her, not since the moment he'd kissed her.

"I guess the way I've been acting made you think I was some kind of—"

"Pushy playboy," Melissa finished for him.

"And here I am a devoted and fairly conservative father, a homebody who mainly photographs kids. Sorry if I gave you the wrong impression."

"That's okay. I made a few silly assumptions all by myself."

The sincere expression in her incredible blue eyes sent his Adam's apple bobbing as he swallowed convulsively. Her pretty mouth curved into a luscious smile and Rafe felt his heart beat a little faster. He'd been giving himself a hard time for being attracted to someone so young, and

46

discovering she was only four years younger than he was was a relief. For the moment, however, he'd better concentrate on his work.

"Well, now that that's cleared up, why don't we try some action shots? Can you walk back and forth between those marks on the floor?"

"Sure."

Gazing through the camera, he took in her delicate features, the soft sweep of hair that looked gold in the bright light. Her small breasts were outlined by her soft sweater, and as she walked her hips swung gracefully beneath the layers of petticoats and skirt. Melissa turned and smiled at the camera's lens. Was she giving him *the* expression again? His body reacting to it, Rafe groped for a safe topic of conversation.

"So you're a teacher, huh? We both have something in common, working with children and all."

"Yes, and you have two beautiful children yourself."

"Aren't they great? They're the best part of my marriage —my ex-marriage, that is. I'm divorced. My wife lives in California now." But he didn't want to talk about Nicole. "Okay, why don't we do some close-ups now? Sit down again."

As Rafe switched to a portrait lens, Melissa repeated, "Your wife lives in California?"

"My ex-wife. I don't have a wife at the moment. Not that I wouldn't like one, but it's hard to find a woman who'll accept a ready-made family." Trying to distract her from asking questions about his disastrous marriage, he jokingly said, "Guess I should put an ad in the paper or something."

"Do you think it would work?"

"Probably not. I need a miracle."

After turning a spotlight directly on her, he moved nearer to adjust her pose. Her eyelashes fluttered as, with one gentle hand, he turned her face toward the light. Her clear skin was as soft as silk and he could see the pulse

47

beating in her throat. Rafe was pleased she didn't try to move away, though her eyes were wide, staring at him. Standing so close, watching her pink lips part as she inhaled, he wanted to cover them with his own. Would she resist?

But any ideas he had were vanquished by the sound of the front door being slammed open.

"Daddy!" Gretta ran across the studio and jumped into his arms. Then the little girl noticed Melissa. "The tooth fairy! How come you're here? I didn't lose another tooth yet."

"I can get rid of one for you, Sis," said Hank, pretending to threaten her as he held up a fist. When he received a stern look from Rafe, he amended, "Aw, I'm just kidding, Dad. I wouldn't hurt her."

"How come you don't have your wings on?" Gretta demanded, running over to Melissa and clutching one of her hands. She reached down to brush at the small girl's bangs.

"They're too heavy to wear every day."

"And what are you doing here with Daddy?"

"Uncle Hux wanted me to take some pictures of her," Rafe explained, grabbing Gretta and tossing her up and down so she squealed with delight. "Before I get back to work and you go upstairs with your grandmother, tell me how school was today."

"We played a pretend game!" Gretta told him excitedly. "We had pretend prizes and stuff and I won! Then we practiced coloring and writing A,B,C. Then I made a phone call."

"To whom?" Rafe frowned as he knelt beside his daughter, holding her loosely within his arms.

"To Mommy," said Gretta. "She said everything was better and we're gonna see her longer this time. We're gonna have some neat Christmas and it's gonna last for lots of days!"

"Don't worry, Dad. She only called from a play phone,"

Hank explained. "They have a bunch of those plastic ones in the first-grade rooms."

Putting his arms around both kids, Rafe led them back toward the entryway and talked to Hank. "I'm not worrying. It's just that I like to be there when you call your mother. I appreciate your keeping an eye on your little sister, son. It makes me proud you're so responsible. How'd everything go with you?"

"Okay. I'm going to put my geography lesson on my computer."

"Will that help?"

"It'll make it more fun. When are you going to get through in here, Dad?" Unsmiling, Hank glanced over his shoulder at Melissa. The look he gave her was significant, almost a glare, and she had a momentary feeling of uneasiness. Was the boy still resentful over the attention afforded his sister the other night?

"I'll be done in time for dinner. In the meantime, why don't you keep your grandmother company? Later, I want to hear more about your schoolwork. Louise!" Rafe yelled as he entered the front hallway.

"Gran brought us home from school and she sweared at a taxi driver!" Gretta babbled loudly.

"I did not swear!" Melissa heard Louise say as the front door opened again, although she couldn't see the older woman from where she was sitting. "I said 'insane beast.' Those are not swear words, Gretta."

Rafe was laughing when he returned. "Aren't they something? I suppose as a father I'm prejudiced, but I often think I've got the smartest, cutest kids in the world."

"They're definitely smart and cute," Melissa agreed. As she made the statement, Rafe beamed with pride.

"I'm going to send them to Harvard," he stated seriously. "Or Princeton or NYU or wherever they want to go. I'll send them to the moon if they want to be astronauts. I'm going to get the best for my kids."

49

"I'm sure most parents feel that way."

"Yeah, parents. But there should be two of them. My kids have only one . . . who can be fully responsible, anyway. They deserve a little extra in other areas." Rafe sighed. "I hope Nicole can take them for the entire two weeks this Christmas. Otherwise, they'll be disappointed like they were last summer when they had to come home early. But I shouldn't complain about all my problems. Wouldn't want to bend your ear."

"Bending is good for my ears. It hones down the points." When Rafe looked at her curiously, Melissa laughed in silvery tones. "I'm a fairy, remember? We all have little pointed ears."

"Let's see." He moved toward her, the expression on his face communicating much more than curiosity. Warmed by his dark liquid gaze, fascinated by the curve of his sensual lips, Melissa caught her breath, wondering just what Rafe intended to examine. Would they recapture the mood they'd started before Gretta's arrival? How disappointing to be interrupted by a childish shout.

"Daddy!" Gretta ran across the studio again. "Come and see the stuff I drew! You come too!" She pointed at Melissa.

"Sweetheart," Rafe said patiently. "We're working. Go back upstairs. I told you I'd talk to you at dinner. Okay?"

Gretta stamped her foot. "No! I want you to look now!"

"Well, all right. But why don't you bring your drawings down here and show us?"

Gretta seemed to consider, then whirled around. "I'm bringing them! I'm bringing them!" she singsonged, skipping out of the studio.

"Sorry for the interruption. We can be quick and finish these shots." He went to work rapidly, having Melissa turn from side to side. They were almost through when Gretta came back.

"Look, Daddy." The little girl presented Rafe with some colorfully scribbled sheets.

"Nice."

"These are very pretty, Gretta," Melissa said when she examined the drawings.

"This is Daddy. This is Mommy. This is a dog. And this," offered Gretta dramatically, waving a paper, "is a big dragon with no teeth!"

As both Rafe and Melissa laughed, Hank walked in. "I thought we were supposed to wait for dinner to talk to you, Dad. How come Gretta's down here?"

"She got impatient."

"Well, if you have time for her, how about coming upstairs with me? You said you'd help me install a new computer program. Or maybe we can play some computer games. I never get to see you very much."

"Yeah, I know. I'm almost finished here."

"Do you suppose we could go out later and look at video recorders? We really need another one, Dad, a machine that can be set for programs at different times on different channels. The other kids at school all have their own." For the first time Hank looked directly at Melissa, giving her a lopsided grin that was a cute version of his father's. She smiled back. "I bet *she'd* like to see some movies with us. Can we buy another one, Dad?"

Listening to Hank's friendly but demanding tone, Melissa saw that Rafe could have a problem with his children. Although they were definitely nice, they were also spoiled. Could he have been indulging them because of his divorce? She remembered what Louise had said about her grandchildren having had a difficult time. Well, it wasn't any of her business. She had enough to think about after discovering Rafe had more sides to him than her initial impression. Although she still thought him forward, she'd seen he was also humorous, intelligent, and good with his children. She'd probably interpreted his teasing remarks as being more than they were.

Observing Rafe helping Gretta pick up the drawings

51

she'd dropped on the floor, Melissa asked, "Are we through? I can go home if you've got other things to do."

"I probably have enough shots."

"We can drive her home and go look at video recorders," suggested Hank.

Melissa went to the hall closet to get her coat. Putting it on and taking out her garment bag, she readied herself to leave.

"Just a moment," Rafe told her from the doorway of the studio, then glanced toward Louise as she suddenly hurried down the stairs.

"Gretta! Hank! Your father is busy now. Come back upstairs. Honestly, I get on the phone for a moment and they disappear."

"Dad's going to take me to look at VCRs," Hank insisted stubbornly.

Placing one arm around his son, Rafe said, "I think it would be better if we went some other time, Hank. Why don't you go upstairs with your grandmother? I'll be up later, like I said."

"Aw, Dad."

"Come on, Gretta," chirped Louise. "I'll bake you some cookies."

"I want cake!"

"We'll make some cupcakes then."

"She's not going to eat her dinner, Louise," Rafe complained.

The older woman sighed. "You know she won't eat any vegetables or meat anyway. I've been giving her cherry-flavored vitamins along with peanut butter for protein."

Rafe shook his head resignedly. "Kids!"

Herding the children up the front stairway, Louise turned to say, "Oh, Rafe, Mr. Feld called and canceled. He wants to make another appointment in a week."

When Melissa started to leave also, Rafe followed her closely. "No more work for today. Hey, how about letting me take you home? As long as it won't offend you, that is. I know I came on a little strong the last time."

"I live only a short distance away—at Twenty-second and Eighth Avenue."

"Please. You'll be doing a poor abused father a favor. I need to get out." He laughed down at her, the expression crinkling the corners of his dark eyes and revealing even, white teeth.

Standing so near him, she once again became aware of his subtle, seductive cologne. Without thinking, she nodded yes.

By the time they reached her apartment building in Chelsea, it was early evening. Light snowflakes drifted down from the dark December sky.

"It was nice enough of you to help me pick up some groceries," Melissa commented as they climbed the winding stairway. "You didn't have to carry them up too."

"Whew!" Rafe huffed, setting down the shopping bags on the fourth-floor landing. "Only two more flights to go. My God, how do you do this every day? Too bad you're not a real fairy. Maybe you could have flown us up."

"I can take the bags from here."

"No, no," Rafe said, resuming his burden. "I need more exercise anyway. And these aren't very heavy."

Although she didn't say so aloud, Melissa was secretly pleased he'd insisted on accompanying her. She was reluctant to give up the warm camaraderie they'd enjoyed since leaving his town house. Could she get him to stay for a cup of tea? Used to relative luxury, would he look down on the way she lived? Surely he could appreciate how she'd fixed up the place and kept it clean.

Still, she experienced a sudden thrill of nervousness when she inserted her keys. The police lock, a huge metal bar that leaned against the door, made a scraping sound as she swung the door open. She switched on the kitchen's

53

overhead bulb by pulling its string. A round white Japanese lantern shaded the light's glare.

"Where shall I put these?"

"On the counter."

"That's a counter?" Rafe stared at the painted wooden planks on top of the bathtub that was placed along one wall of the tiny room.

"As long as I'm not taking a bath. This is one of those old buildings that was originally erected without bathroom plumbing. The tub was added later, along with a water closet. See?" Melissa opened a door to reveal the toilet. She'd painted the tall, narrow space a soft rose and covered its six-foot window with a narrow bamboo blind. "You can catch a great view of the Empire State Building from here."

"How entertaining."

"I like it," Melissa stated, trying not to be defensive. "I'll show you the rest of the place. It's a railroad apartment, with one room opening right into another." She led him through the other three small rooms, turning on the lanterns she'd rigged up as lights. The last room fronted the street six floors below and also featured a magnificent view of the Empire State Building. Tonight its glowing lights were somewhat dimmed by the steady descent of snow.

"I grew some flowers out on the fire escape last summer." Could she really expect him to admire her ingenuity? Should she ask him how he liked the way she'd painted the rooms in soft white and decorated them with careful choices of second-hand furniture? Would he be impressed that she'd refinished the rocking chair herself and made a tablecloth for the cheap card table? Did he appreciate the delicate touches she'd added—dried flowers and pretty stones, candles of every shape and size imaginable? If so, would it mean he really liked *her?*

"Very nice," he said noncommittally, looking around. "I haven't seen a place like this in a long time." When she

54

raised her brows in question, he explained, "I have some friends who used to live in a similar apartment in the East Village." On their way back to the kitchen, he eyed her futon mattress lying on the floor. "And I haven't seen furniture of this sort since I was in college."

"Furniture of what sort?"

"The kind that's impermanent, lightweight."

"Oh? Do you think I should carry a sleeper sofa up to the sixth floor?"

"You've got a point there." He grinned as he walked over to her bags of groceries. "I'll help you put these away."

"No, you've done enough. Why don't you let me fix you some tea?"

"Can you get near enough to the stove to do it?" he wondered, examining the small, old appliance that sat behind one end of the tub.

"I can get in to use the burners. I just can't open the oven door completely."

"Luckily, you're tiny." For a moment, he raked his gaze over her appreciatively. "You're lovely too. I neglected to tell you that when I was taking your pictures today and teased you by calling you cute." He moved closer, speaking softly. "Actually, Melissa, I don't have time for tea. But I'd like to look at your ears before I go. I didn't get the chance before. Are they really pointed?" Placing his hands in her hair, he caressed the silky strands and gazed deeply into her eyes.

They moved naturally into a kiss, Melissa fitting neatly into his hard, compact body. His lips warm and tender, he explored her own with soft pressure. Closing her eyelids tightly and murmuring deep in her throat, she laced her arms securely about his neck, trying to get even closer. Rafe responded by kissing her more deeply.

When their tongues touched, sweet sensations spiraled out from her center and she felt lost, as if she had fallen into a magical realm of airy darkness. Were they both falling?

Briefly, Melissa envisioned herself and Rafe drifting high above the lighted city, gliding softly through the night like snowflakes on the wind. Would her fragile wings be enough to break their steep descent?

His warm hands moving up her sides awakened her. She gasped as his palms cupped the underside of her breasts, then moved back to her waist. Gently, he held her away from him. "I think I'd better go," Rafe said huskily. "Or I'm never going to get home for dinner tonight."

"Perhaps you should." Her initial disappointment turned quickly into appreciation. This man was definitely not the playboy she'd first thought.

"It's not that I want to leave," Rafe told her sincerely. "Can I see you again?"

"I'd like that."

They moved apart awkwardly, Melissa not knowing what to do with her hands. Finally, she clasped them behind her back. Would that keep her from reaching out to touch him again?

"I'll call you," he promised.

When he left Melissa leaned over the railing of the stairwell and watched him descend six flights to the main floor below. He waved up to her, then disappeared. Humming to herself, she reentered her apartment and stood quietly for a while, looking out of the front room's tall windows. It was snowing harder now. Perhaps by morning New York would be transformed into a lovely winter wonderland. Something wonderful had already transpired for Melissa. Was her casual wish for romance—jokingly expressed to Clarence—really about to come true? Would the negative image she'd had of Rafe dissolve into one of exactly the kind of man she was looking for?

"Once upon a time," she began. "There was a handsome prince and a beautiful fairy. And it was winter and the snow was falling all around . . ." Melissa laughed. She couldn't help herself. "And then they fell in love and even-

56

tually they got married and lived happily ever after in a beautiful castle that was decorated with snowflakes in winter and flowers in summer." Wasn't that the way all fairy tales went?

Unfortunately, though, life was not a fairy tale. Willing herself to be more serious, Melissa realized she was making a lot of playful assumptions considering she and Rafe hardly knew each other and hadn't even gone out yet.

What if he never called? Frowning, she quickly pushed the negative thought aside. They'd felt so right together, just as their sizes made kissing thoroughly enjoyable. She'd always been annoyed when a man had to pull her up on the tips of her toes in order to kiss her, sometimes lifting her completely off her feet. Rafe Damon was just about perfect.

Almost skipping toward the kitchen, her holiday spirits surging, Melissa sang a Christmas carol as she fixed herself some dinner.

CHAPTER FOUR

" 'So the bearded troll made his home under the Brooklyn Bridge, just as he'd threatened to do,' " Melissa said in a low tone, widening her eyes as she peered around at the enthralled group of seven- and eight-year-old-children. " 'He made everyone who wanted to use the bridge pay a very costly toll.' That means people had to pay a lot of money," she explained.

"What did he do if they didn't have any money?"

"Why, he would frighten them, of course," Melissa told the blond girl who had already put her thumb back in her mouth. "He was a very mean and greedy troll."

She ducked her head to read from the open storybook in her hands, lifting her eyes every sentence or so to make sure the children were paying attention. She had no need to worry; they were a captive audience, hanging on to every dramatic word until the conclusion of the story.

" 'And so, when he tried to scare the old lady, the troll barely escaped being run over by a speeding car. "It's not safe! It's not safe!" he yelled as he stomped up and down, trying to shake the bridge so it would sway. That's when the troll decided to return to his home in the big hollow tree in Central Park where he would mine gold to make fine jewelry like his ancestors before him.' " Melissa closed the book. A movement caught her eye, and she saw Rafe watching her from a short distance away. "Did anyone learn something from this story?"

"I know!" yelled a dark-haired boy as he wildly waved his hand. "Don't play in traffic or you might get runned over."

The girl next to him punched his arm and told him, "It's supposed to be nobody likes you if you're mean."

"Naw! There's gold buried in Central Park!" shouted another child.

"You have a very good imagination, Anthony," Melissa said, laughing. "But if there was gold in Central Park, someone would have found it long ago." Trying not to let Rafe's presence interfere with her work, Melissa continued the dissection of the story and was amused by the diverse opinions of her young audience. As always, she led a discussion meant to inspire them to want to know more, which meant developing reading skills. "Now, who wants to check out this book?"

"Me!"

"Me!"

Luckily, Melissa had more than one copy. Small hands grabbed those as well as other books the children could take home. "You all have your library cards?" Heads nodded solemnly as several reached into their pockets to find them. "All right, go ahead, but no pushing in line."

The children waved as they headed for the checkout desk.

" 'Bye, Miss Ryan."

"See you next week."

"Enjoy your stories," Melissa said, waving back.

"A troll, huh?" Rafe sauntered forward. "Nothing to say about fairies today?"

"I use any kind of story that I think is appropriate for the group and that will go with the books available on a particular week. The children seem to enjoy the variety."

"I enjoy fairies myself," Rafe said, his dark eyes roaming her shoulders as though he were looking for her wings. When he moved closer Melissa laughed a little nervously and shied away.

59

"I have clean-up detail before I leave," she told him, stooping to pick up a stray piece of paper. "It will just take me a few minutes. I have to put these books back on the shelves."

"No hurry. I enjoy watching you flit around."

That statement, of course, made her more nervous. Melissa was already torn about going out with the man. She'd convinced herself Rafe was no playboy and that he had more going for him than that, but how could she be sure? He'd wasted no time in calling her, doing so from the deli down the street right after leaving her place the night before. Last night she'd thought the call flattering. Now she was wondering if Rafe wasn't moving a little too fast.

When they walked out of the Midtown library she thought her suspicions were confirmed when he suggested they grab an early dinner at an intimate little restaurant down the street.

"I—I'm not really hungry yet. Couldn't we walk around for a little while and talk or something? Maybe we could eat later."

"Anything you want," Rafe told her, his smile making her pulse flutter. Melissa clasped her hands behind her back as they walked down the street and was pleasantly surprised when he talked about her work. "You were really something in there, you know. You had those kids eating out of your hand and loving every minute."

"That's what M.R.F. is all about." He looked puzzled, so she explained, "Making Reading Fun. It's a new federally funded reading enrichment program that encourages kids to read early. Right now I've got five- to eight-year-olds, but a few of the other teachers start with kids as young as two."

"They teach two-year-old kids to read?"

"Not exactly. What they do is develop reading readiness."

As they walked on, Melissa found herself relaxing in

Rafe's company, so that by the time they got to Fifth Avenue, she'd told him all about her hectic work schedule, running to two libraries a day on Tuesday, Wednesday, and Saturday while playing sugarplum fairy on Monday, Thursday, and Sunday, and about the roommate who'd eloped the month before, making both jobs necessary to Melissa's survival.

"I really love my job with M.R.F., but one part-time job doesn't pay the bills. If I'm lucky, one of these days I'll find a full-time position that will give me the same satisfaction."

She'd grown so comfortable with Rafe she hadn't even noticed exactly when he'd taken her arm, but the gesture was comforting, especially when she slipped on a patch of ice and he prevented her from falling. Then his grip tightened. Imagining she could feel the warmth of his hand right through her thick down jacket made Melissa feel more jittery than secure, however.

They window-shopped down the avenue, eventually reaching Rockefeller Center. Continuing past the angels along the promenade, they headed for the ice-skating rink with its golden guardian, the gigantic statue of Prometheus, and the towering Christmas tree above and behind it. Carefully putting some space between herself and Rafe, Melissa admired the colored lights on the tree and watched the skaters on the frozen plaza below with a touch of nostalgia.

"I used to ice-skate on a frozen pond on our farm when I was a kid. I hadn't realized I missed it."

"We could skate now, if you like."

Glancing at his expensive leather coat and wool slacks and at her own full apricot-colored skirt, she laughed. "I don't think either one of us is appropriately dressed. Why don't we plan to skate some other time when we're better prepared? Maybe we could bring your kids."

Rafe smiled at the suggestion. "Really? You wouldn't mind taking the kids with us sometime?"

"Really. I'm from a close family, myself. As a matter of fact, I taught my two little brothers to skate—well, they're not so little now, and they might not admit I taught them anything, but I did."

"Gretta and Hank would love it if we took them skating. So would I, Melissa. You don't know how thrilled I am to meet a woman who doesn't mind my family ties."

"I guess I miss my own," she admitted.

They watched the skaters a little longer, Melissa drifting comfortably closer to Rafe as he put his arm around her shoulders. Once more she experienced the feeling that they were perfect for each other; their interest in and work with kids, the way they fit together physically.

Then her mind naughtily wandered to more intimate ways in which they might fit together. Fluttering excitement crept through her, bringing on a heated blush. Melissa ducked her head away from Rafe, not wanting him to guess the sensual wanderings of her mind. But then, did she have to worry? So far, he hadn't been in the least pushy. It seemed like those kinds of ideas were all in her own head, not in his.

"Maybe we should get something to eat," she blurted suddenly, trying to distract herself from continuing to fantasize about a man she hardly knew.

"I thought you'd never mention food," Rafe said, something like gratitude reflected in his sexy eyes, making her feel giddy. "My poor, abused stomach thanks you. I was so busy this morning that I didn't have time to grab lunch. I was half-starved when I picked you up at the library."

Melissa flushed guiltily, remembering it was her paranoia about his questionable intentions that had prevented Rafe from eating. Now it was she who had the ideas. She immediately agreed to go to a restaurant several blocks away.

While they ate it was Rafe's turn to talk about his job and how he'd apprenticed and then become partners with his father. "When he died Louise said she didn't want to be alone. So we renovated the whole place and moved in with her."

Melissa was sure "we" included Nicole as well as the children. It made her brave enough to ask, "Why does your ex-wife live in California?" What she really wanted to know was why he, rather than his ex-wife, had custody.

To her frustration he avoided saying anything of substance. "Nicole is still trying to find herself. She took a job in California last summer, but I wouldn't be surprised if it doesn't last and she moves on. She's always liked changes, especially when they're unexpected."

"Sometimes the unexpected is fun, but I guess it must be hard on the kids."

"Nicole loves Gretta and Hank as much as I do."

From the closed look on his face, she could tell the subject was better left alone, but the fact that he didn't make disparaging remarks about his ex-wife made Rafe a pretty nice man in Melissa's opinion. That fact, added to his more obvious physical attraction, appealed to her, and yet she was reluctant to rush things. So when they finished their meal and he would have flagged down a taxi, she suggested they walk to her place.

Once on their way, Melissa couldn't stop herself from anticipating the delicious things that could happen when they got there. This time she chastised herself for such imaginings much more reluctantly. It wasn't as if she had similar thoughts about every man she dated. To Melissa, Rafe was the unexpected.

Following that thought, something unexpected did happen: A sewer cover popped up in the street, the noise startling Melissa into stopping. A shaggy head slowly rose above street level, then turned toward her and Rafe. An old man with a long beard crooked a filthy finger directly at her.

"He looks like one of those trolls you told the kids about.

Maybe he wants to charge us to use the city sidewalks," Rafe whispered humorously.

"Psst!" The grubby man crooked his finger again. Melissa stepped toward him, pulling her arm free from Rafe's grasp, ignoring his exasperated protest. "Can you spare a buck, lady?" Sympathy for someone in poorer circumstances than she prompted Melissa to open her purse and pull out five dollars. It was almost Christmas, wasn't it? After grabbing and inspecting the bill, the old man yelled, "Thanks!" Then his head bobbed down and the sewer cover was pulled back into place.

"Aren't you concerned for your own safety, Melissa?" Rafe asked reprovingly as she turned back to him with a broad smile on her face. "How did you know that old bum wouldn't hurt you?"

Her smile faded. "Rafe! He's only a poor troll trying to make a living." She thought he would laugh at that, but he scowled instead. Melissa frowned in return.

"More likely he's an old wino and your generosity will be wasted on a bottle. Besides, I thought you needed money."

Where was Rafe's sense of humor? Melissa wondered. Her action obviously annoyed him, but she couldn't understand why since he didn't seem to be ungenerous. Could the responsibility of a family have made him overly practical? His shift in moods put a pall over the evening. They barely spoke for the next few blocks before he relaxed and took her arm.

Soon he had her amused with stories of his kids, and the evening ahead seemed to open with possibilities once more. She practically skipped up the six flights of steps while Rafe trudged behind her. But when they reached her landing and Melissa unlocked her door, he leaned against the doorjamb, puffing heavily.

"I hate to leave your charming company, but I'm beat, Melissa." He touched her lips with his fingers. "It's been a long day and I have an early shoot tomorrow morning."

"On Sunday?" She tried to keep the disappointment from her voice.

"I'm afraid so. The holidays are hectic in my business." He kissed her softly and backed off. "I'll call you."

Would he really? "Thanks for dinner," she said brightly. "I enjoyed myself."

Melissa entered her apartment, locking the door behind her. Thoughtfully, she made her way to the front room. Looking down, she watched until Rafe left her building and disappeared down the street. Had he really left because he was tired? Or because she gave an old bum some money? Or maybe he found her boring?

The last seemed most likely. Melissa knew she couldn't compete with the beautiful models he must meet when he wasn't working with children. Rather than being glad he hadn't tried to push her into intimacy, Melissa was worried that he hadn't seemed to want to. Where was her magic fairy dust when she needed it? She went to bed after convincing herself Rafe Damon would never call her.

But he did, the very next day, bolstering Melissa's sagging spirits. They made plans to see each other later that week and to take the kids skating on the following weekend. She was looking forward to their next encounter with delicious anticipation.

"Rafe's going to be late tonight," Louise explained as she stacked plates into the dishwasher. "It's already six and he's not finished. He often runs overtime on Saturdays."

"I know. We planned to go out for only a short while."

Seating herself at the butcher-block table which served as the kitchen's work island, Melissa decided she'd be glad when the holidays were over and Rafe's work load would slow down. Getting together during the past few weeks had proven to be a scheduling feat for them both. She hoped Rafe would still have energy to go dancing tonight.

"You're not bored keeping me company?" the older

woman asked, closing the dishwasher door and turning it on. "I'm sure it's not amusing to watch me clean up after the kids' dinner."

"Don't be silly, Louise. I enjoy seeing you and the children. I like the atmosphere in this house. Say, would you like help cleaning up?"

"Stay where you are. I'm almost finished."

Melissa had spoken truthfully when she'd said she enjoyed being in Rafe's house. Their casual dates the past few weeks—sometimes including the children—had brought her into contact with his family many times. Arriving at his place after work, she'd either go out with Rafe or spend the better part of an evening merely talking and laughing with him on his living-room couch.

"We enjoy your company too," Louise echoed Melissa's sentiments, smiling as she adjusted a framed photograph of the kids that hung above the sink. Showing them at a younger age, the print was one of the few that hung among the gleaming utensils and decorative baskets on the walls in the pleasant natural wood and blue-toned kitchen.

Louise was sincere, but Melissa wondered if the woman could speak for Rafe's children. Although he'd seemed very careful about foisting his girlfriend on them and vice versa, Melissa knew they were looking her over, especially Hank. By turns the boy had been friendly and distant. Would he grow to accept her?

Running her hands thoughtfully over the table's smooth wood, Melissa told herself it was much too soon to worry about it. She and Rafe hadn't dated very long—they hadn't even made love yet—and here she was entertaining thoughts of becoming a stepmother. She grinned. When they'd first met she'd thought Rafe was a playboy. Now his slow pace was making her impatient.

"Would you like a cup of coffee?" Louise asked. Melissa shook her head at the same time Gretta came galloping down the stairs toward them.

Rafe's daughter pranced into the kitchen. "I got somethin' new to show you, Melissa. Guess what? I got a set of pretty new paints! My friend Peggy gave 'em to me!"

"I'd like to see them." Melissa hugged her, hardly noticing the change in the child's appearance.

But Louise did. "Gretta! What have you done to your bangs?"

Melissa stared too. The little girl's usual hairdo was cut short in front, or rather chopped off in varying lengths, some locks almost standing on end.

"It got in my eyes," Gretta complained.

"I told you I was going to trim it. Why didn't you ask me?"

"I waited but you didn't have time."

"I did so. You simply got impatient. What a mess!" Louise took Gretta's head in her hands to survey the damage. Melissa thought the other woman was more abrupt than she'd usually be with her granddaughter. "Your hair is ruined. How can I put you on a plane tomorrow and send you to your mother like this? You've been a bad girl! What shall we do?"

"It's ruint?"

"You're going to look awful." Louise seized a brush from a nearby shelf and then grabbed the child. "Honestly, do I have to hide all the scissors? What got into you, Gretta?"

"I ruint my hair?" Gretta's eyes filled with tears. The unexpected disapproval from Louise was upsetting her. "Can't I go see Mommy anyway?" As Louise held up strands from her ravaged bangs and frowned, Gretta began to cry in earnest. "I didn't mean to," she wailed.

Melissa's heart was touched. "Let me look at it," she told Louise. "I'm pretty good at cutting hair. Maybe I can do something." Kneeling beside Gretta, she said softly, "Don't worry, sweetie. We'll fix it this time, but you shouldn't try to cut your hair by yourself, you know."

"I won't do it again, I promise. Can I still go see Mommy?"

"I didn't say you couldn't see your mom," Louise told the little girl. "I only want you to look nice for her."

"And we'll make sure you look extra nice," Melissa said assuringly, leading Gretta down the hall to the bathroom and winking at Louise as the older woman followed to hand her a pair of scissors.

It took some clever work, but Melissa trimmed what remained of Gretta's bangs into layers slanting across her temples. "Like it?" she asked the child as she tried to blend a few impossibly short strands into the style.

"It's different."

"But we girls like to try different styles, don't we? Maybe you'll start a new fashion."

"I will?"

"Of course. You can wear it this way now and then let it grow back again or try something even newer. Just make sure you let your Gran cut it when you want to change your hairstyle."

"Or you?"

"Sure." Melissa almost added "if I'm here," but thought better of it.

"How cute!" Louise peeked inside the bathroom. When Gretta ran outside to admire herself in a full-length mirror, she lowered her voice. "Thanks. It looks good. Actually, I'd put off doing Gretta's hair because I'm so bad with haircuts. I thought Nicole would trim it in California." Smiling, she headed back toward the kitchen as the phone rang.

"Let's go upstairs!" Gretta had regained her good humor.

Noticing that Louise was sitting at the kitchen table talking on the phone, Melissa followed the child upstairs, Gretta trying to take two steps at a time. The little girl had made a ritual of showing Melissa any of her new possessions since the first time she'd arrived at the house to go out to dinner with Rafe. Now Gretta led the way into her room past shelves of dolls and plush animals that she'd already introduced by age and name, past full toy boxes, to a pile of papers spread out over her small desk.

Shuffling a stack of drawing paper and a few coloring books aside, Gretta said, "Here they are!" She held up a package of brightly colored poster paints. "Want me to make you a picture?"

"I'd like that," agreed Melissa. "But don't you think we'd better go downstairs? Paints can be messy."

"I want to paint here," the child insisted.

"You might spill paint on your rug or your bed."

"I'm gonna paint here!" Gretta raised her voice.

Taken aback, Melissa decided to try a different tactic. "Well, okay. But the kitchen table is lots bigger than your desk. You could do a really big picture there."

"Yeah? A really, really big one?"

Melissa was happy Gretta finally agreed and gathered up some paper to bring along. If only the little girl hadn't been used to getting her own way so frequently. From what she'd gathered from Louise and Rafe, things had not always been like this. Both adults felt sorry for the child, who had cried at night for months after her mother left. Unfortunately, their desire to grant her every wish was severely spoiling her.

In the hallway Melissa glanced toward Hank's doorway, listening to the clicking sounds issuing from within.

"That's Hank's computer," Gretta said proudly. "He's smart."

"I know." Rafe had told Melissa about the high grades his son always brought home from school.

"Want to see it?" Not waiting for an answer, Gretta grabbed Melissa's hand and pulled her through the door.

Seated at a long, modern wood desk, Hank warily looked

up from the green screen of his computer monitor. Above the desk were myriad shelves filled with books, software, various sports equipment, and what looked like a mounted bug collection. Above the shelves a three-foot replica of a jet plane hung from wires.

"I came to show Melissa your machine!" Gretta exclaimed.

"I've got lots of machines," Hank said.

"Then show her all of 'em."

Melissa took in the rows of robots and other mechanical toys. The bedroom was large, with three built-in carpeted levels in an L-shape against two walls. Each tier held different items—a built-in mattress, a portable color television, a cordless telephone, the robots, a small stereo, and various other electronic devices. The luxurious room was almost as big as Melissa's apartment.

Pointing at the robots, Gretta asked, "Do you like 'em?"

"Aw. She's not interested, Gretta."

"Yes I am."

"Well, I like my computer better than toys now."

"That's interesting too."

"Really? Want to see my Treasure Hunt computer game? It teaches you history while you play."

Eager to encourage Hank's friendly gesture, Melissa pulled up another chair to watch and sat down with Gretta on her lap. The boy pointed out the logistics of the game, then told her about his word-processing and mathematics software.

"Good grief!" Melissa finally said. "You're going to be ready for a computer programming job before you graduate from junior high."

Hank grinned broadly, obviously pleased at her flattery. "I bet I'm ready now. Everyone says I'm smart enough to do anything I want. Only I don't want to be a programmer. I want to design these machines. See?" He reached over to pick up a small robot, twisting and turning its parts around. "This robot can be transformed to look like a truck or a plane. I want to design computers that can transform too— maybe into real cars."

"Sounds great," Melissa said.

"As soon as Dad buys me a modem, I'm going to hook up with data banks. Then I can get lots of information on designing."

"Daddy said you don't need a modem," Gretta objected. "He said you got too much stuff already."

"I'll get one." Hank sounded confident, then gave Melissa what she thought was a crafty look. "He'll change his mind."

Since Gretta had begun squirming restlessly, Melissa suggested they go paint. Hank accompanied them to the stairs, talking about his design plans. Though his ideas were as farfetched as those of a normal eleven-year-old, she could imagine she was conversing with a more mature boy. That illusion was aided by the fact that he was already taller than Melissa.

Louise helped them get set up at the kitchen table. Spreading newspapers down, she filled two cups with water. "Now, don't paint too long, Gretta. I'm going to take you over to Aunt Shirley's. Then we'll go get some ice cream and you can stay up later tonight."

"Yea!" Gretta cried, swinging her brush above her head. Luckily it hadn't been dipped into a paint jar yet.

"Sure you want to do this now?" Melissa asked.

"I want to do lots of pictures fast. Want me to paint a dragon?"

"You could, but how about something to do with Christmas? That day's coming up later this week. Aren't you excited?"

"Yeah! I'll paint Santa Claus." Uninhibited, Gretta picked up a sheet and proceeded to paint a large purple circle with a small green body and red dots for eyes.

71

"Is that Santa?"

"No, it's me!" Gretta informed her. Melissa laughed as the child put a smaller figure in the corner and pronounced that it was Santa, then told her what presents he was carrying in his sack.

What fun it was to work creatively with children! That's why Melissa enjoyed her job with the library so much. And there were no discipline problems like there had been at the public school.

"This is you." Gretta drew Melissa's attention back by pointing to a tiny red blob at the edge of the page.

"Very nice," commented Melissa, flattered the child had thought to include her. She hoped both of Rafe's kids would like the Christmas gifts she planned to give them before she left tonight.

"And now I'm going to make another picture." Gretta grabbed a clean sheet and slapped yellow paint on it. "Do you know what this is? Californ'ya. I'm gonna go there tomorrow. And guess what? I made a real big wish to Santa." Gretta drew circles and added arms and legs. "See? This is Daddy and this is Mommy. I wished they'd be back together again."

Melissa's smile froze, but Gretta wasn't paying attention. They both turned when Rafe walked into the kitchen.

"Hey, my two lovely ladies. I finally finished all the work down there. Saved up some hugs and kisses for a tired man?" Embracing Gretta, he grinned at Melissa over his daughter's head.

"Hi, Rafe." She hoped there wasn't a suspicious look on her face. Thrown off balance by Gretta's painting and announcement, she wondered if Rafe actually ever planned on getting back with Nicole. Was that why he didn't talk about his ex-wife? Were they still in love? Was that the real reason he'd never made love to Melissa? Or was she merely reacting insecurely to something any child whose parents had divorced would say?

Giving Gretta and her father the benefit of the doubt, Melissa rose, aware the little girl was watching, and offered Rafe a sedate, welcoming kiss.

CHAPTER FIVE

Later, holding Melissa in his arms as they relaxed on the huge sectional sofa in the living room, Rafe wondered why she'd acted a little strange when he'd first seen her tonight. Was she annoyed because he'd pleaded exhaustion and ordered out for pizza instead of taking her to dinner at a restaurant? He knew he hadn't been courting her the way a man was supposed to. Unfortunately, December was one of his busiest months and they'd both had unusual schedules.

"I'm sorry I don't feel like going out tonight."

"We didn't make definite plans," Melissa said. "And it's nice to curl up and watch the fire." She gazed into the flames burning in the brick fireplace before them, then turned her head toward the decorated tree in one corner of the room. "Your Christmas tree is pretty to look at too. When did you put it up?"

"Last night." Rafe nuzzled her soft cheek, cradling her shoulders in the crook of his arm. The ivory silk of her antique blouse felt slippery beneath his fingers and he noticed the lacy edge of an undergarment revealed by the garment's low neck—as well as a few inches of creamy flesh. Repressing his natural reaction to her innocent sensuality, he said, "As far as going out, I promise I'll make it up to you. I've had one heck of a work schedule the last few weeks. I wouldn't ordinarily ask a date to casually drop by my place."

"What do you usually ask women to do?"

"Well," Rafe began jokingly, "it might be too naughty to tell."

"You've been doing naughty things with other women?" Melissa pouted.

Rafe laughed. "You don't need to be jealous. I've rarely gone out with anyone more than once or twice in the past two years. I couldn't find a woman I wanted to see more than that. And, despite your former ideas about me being a swinging single, you know I'm a regular homebody. I'd rather lie around on a couch and talk than go to some club."

"And order out for pizza, right?"

"Yeah, but I plan to take you to a dozen places next week when we both have more time." Melissa had told him she'd be on vacation from her job next week.

"I enjoy seeing you in any situation." Melissa gave him a feathery kiss that, despite his state of exhaustion, made his pulse race. He kissed her in return, then nestled his head against hers.

In reality he'd like nothing better than to fill his stomach with food and retire for the night—with Melissa beside him. Then they could have the pleasure of waking together too. Of course that was impossible since the kids would be coming home with Louise later on. And Melissa would probably be offended if he suggested it. No woman liked to go to a man's house and go straight to bed. Rafe didn't want to rush her; he was hoping to build her trust before they became intimate.

"Did you see Gretta's paintings tonight?" she asked.

Rafe yawned. "I wasn't paying much attention, but she showed me some wild-looking stuff. Those kids have so much energy. We stayed up late last night decorating the Christmas tree—it was our last evening alone before they leave. And they've kept me going all week with their jabbering and packing. They're both so excited about going to see Nicole, they've hardly been able to sleep. I only hope it turns out all right this time."

"They had some problems their last trip?"

He thought it was time he explained a few things about his ex-wife. "Nicole's always had difficulty knowing exactly what she wants. She skips from one thing to another. Since the divorce she's had several jobs and moved twice. Last summer the kids came home early when she had to move to a different city because of her newest career plans. They were very upset."

"It takes children some time to adjust to a divorce."

"I guess so." Rafe didn't want to tell her how nervous the approaching trip had made him. Part of his present fatigue was due to his worry about his kids and the journey that would take them so far away from him. "At least I can count on Hank to take good care of his sister."

She gazed at him earnestly. "It's none of my business, but have you ever thought of getting back together with Nicole?"

Why was she asking him a question like that? "Are you kidding? We married too young and were never suited for each other in the first place. She wanted to party and jump from interest to interest. I wanted to nest. I'll be happy if she can settle down and make a permanent place for the kids to stay when they visit her."

Had she asked about his ex-wife because she was getting serious about him? Rafe was afraid to ask, but he was hopeful. Although they hadn't known one another very long, he was sure he could get serious about Melissa. But even so, he was taking things slowly. Tending to be intense when his passions were aroused, he didn't want to scare her away.

Half reclining against the thick upholstered back of the couch, he felt his eyelids start to droop. "Rafe?" His eyes blinked open when Melissa pulled herself up and placed her arms around his neck. "I'm sure everything will turn out okay. I have a good feeling about it."

"Going to do some fairy magic?"

Instead of answering that question, she produced another kind of magic by placing her mouth on his. Lashes lowered provocatively, she gave him soft, exploratory kisses. His sluggish blood sped up when her small tongue slid over his half-open lips and her palms moved inside his shirt to caress his bare chest.

Accepting her mouth eagerly, he turned to fold her into a more complete embrace. She melted against him with a drawn-out sigh. The expression of satisfaction aroused him even further. Becoming aware of each sweet place their bodies touched, he deepened their kiss and placed one firm hand against her hips, drawing her closer.

Running a questing hand over her silky blouse, he felt her warm flesh quiver underneath. His exploring fingers slipped inside the blouse, several of its tiny buttons unfastening of their own accord. Beneath the lace of her camisole, he felt her nipples spring to life, hardening at his touch. Lovingly, he moved the material of the undergarment aside, then broke their kiss. She made a slight sound when his mouth moved to her breast.

Suddenly he heard a loud buzzing. He tried to ignore it, but the instrusive sound reverberated again and again.

"The doorbell!" Rafe exclaimed angrily, normal consciousness penetrating his passionate haze. "Damn! Is that the pizza already?"

"Probably. Aren't you hungry anymore?"

He gazed into her clouded eyes. "I'm hungry all right, but I want a lot more than food now."

"Me too," she murmured. They stared at one another, hair and clothing disheveled. Rafe reached out to draw her close again.

But the doorbell continued to ring. Cursing, Rafe got off the couch to slip on his shoes. Glancing back at Melissa reluctantly, he hurried down to the floor below.

Tucking her stockinged feet beneath her, she took several deep breaths to get herself together, then began to straighten her blouse. It was then that she heard it. In the quiet of the living room, underlying the gentle sound of the fire's crackling, there was a faint but definite whirring or humming. Was an appliance running somewhere in the room? Fastening a button, she looked around. The sound was definitely nearby. In fact, it seemed to be coming from below.

Leaning over, Melissa inserted a hand beneath the couch and her fingers touched something cool and solid. Filled with curiosity, she grasped the strange object and pulled out a tape recorder. Quickly shutting it off, she traced the cord connected to the machine to the cushion beneath her. At its end was a micro switch. Although she wasn't an expert in electronics, it didn't take her long to figure things out. Obviously, someone had rigged up a clever spying device. The tape recorder had been set to run when she and Rafe sat on their usual place on the couch. The attached pressure-sensitive switch turned it on as their weight pressed against the cushions.

And Melissa knew who'd set the trap; it had to be Hank. She was sure the intelligent boy was capable of figuring out such a scheme. He must be watching her more suspiciously than she thought, wanting to hear what his father and his girlfriend were talking about—or doing. She was appalled at the idea. And he'd almost gotten away with it. Should she tell Rafe? she wondered.

Spontaneously deciding against it, and knowing Rafe would be back soon, Melissa took action to destroy the evidence. Rewinding the tape, she set the machine on record again. Then she placed the battery-operated device back under the couch where it would record over and thus erase the previous audio.

"Melissa?" Rafe stood in the doorway with the pizza box in his hand.

"Why don't we eat in the kitchen?" she suggested, flush-

78

ing slightly. That would be too far for the recorder to pick up their conversation.

"I guess we should. I'd rather continue with what we were doing but Louise and the kids could be home at any time." He grinned wryly. After rising to kiss him lightly on the lips, Melissa led him into the other room.

While they ate the pepperoni and mushroom pizza, she once again toyed with the idea of telling Rafe about Hank, but couldn't bring herself to do it. That kind of action was against her principles. What if she, an outsider to the family, started trouble between the father and son? Hank might just be going through a normal stage brought on by his anxiety about his parents' divorce. Surely given time and love, he'd come around.

Hank certainly had better things to do than spy on his dad, Melissa thought, remembering all the toys and amusements she'd seen in the kid's room. Where had he gotten so much stuff? She hoped Rafe didn't indulge his son by buying him anything he wanted. Love that didn't include discipline was never going to help the boy grow. Surely Hank had been wishfully thinking when he'd said he'd get his dad to buy him a computer modem. The boy probably did that a lot, she decided, recalling the day in the studio when his son had nagged Rafe for a video recorder. Had Hank already forgotten about that costly item?

Between bites of pizza she asked curiously, "Did you and Hank ever go to look at the video recorder he wanted?"

"No, but I bought him a new one for Christmas."

"What a nice present," Melissa said, almost gulping her food down the wrong way. "Expensive, though."

"Yeah, I know. I'm going to give it to him when he gets back from California. Now he wants a modem for his computer too. I suppose being able to obtain data-base information would make it worthwhile and help him with his studies."

"You're going to buy him one?"

"I'm thinking about it."

Melissa grew quiet and willed herself not to intervene. The way Rafe chose to raise his children was none of her business—at least not at the moment. In the coming week she'd be on vacation from her library job and she was hoping since she couldn't go home and had already told her folks as much, that she and Rafe could spend a lot of time together, certainly Christmas Eve and Christmas. Their burgeoning relationship should take on new and deeper dimensions, including the physical. Just thinking about the kisses they'd shared on his couch tonight was enough to make her toes tingle.

"Boy, am I tired." Putting aside his plate, Rafe yawned again. "Now that I've eaten, I could fall asleep on my feet. Maybe a night's rest will revive me. I'm glad the kids are taking a late-morning flight."

"Should I leave now?" Melissa asked. Perhaps it was best, but she couldn't help feeling disappointed. Although she'd already given up the idea of going dancing, she'd hoped they could spend more time together.

Rafe squeezed her hand. "Don't go yet. I'll drive you home after Louise gets back with the car."

"But you're so tired."

"I'll last an hour longer. Thinking about how much I'll see you next week will give me energy."

Imagining how she'd enjoy Christmas with him, Melissa smiled. Maybe he could help her put up a tree.

"In fact, you know, we could start our togetherness tomorrow."

"What do you have in mind?" she asked eagerly.

"Why don't we drive up the coast? Maybe we could stop at a nice country inn for a few days. All alone in the country. Wouldn't that be nice?"

"Tomorrow?" Was that his Christmas plan?

"You're on vacation now, right?"

"I'm on vacation from my library job, but I'm still working at the store until Christmas Eve—Tuesday. That's the end of that position."

"The kooky sugarplum fairy job?" Rafe frowned.

Melissa tried not to be annoyed. "Right, the kooky job that pays part of my rent."

"Damn. I thought you had tomorrow off."

"No, but I'm off tomorrow night, late Monday night, Tuesday night, and Chris—"

"But that doesn't help our plans for going out of town. I have to be home on Wednesday when the kids will call."

Was the most important thing to him being home on Christmas for his kids' call? Why couldn't he call them from wherever he might be? Gulping down the lump in her throat, she suddenly felt guilty. If she voiced her thoughts she'd sound like she was jealous of his children. But didn't he care anything about spending the holiday with her? What did it matter if they went out of town? Being together was the most important thing.

"I don't understand why you don't look for a regular full-time job," Rafe went on. "What would be so bad about it?"

"I have looked for a full-time job, Rafe," Melissa said, annoyed that he was changing the subject instead of making plans for the holidays. "I simply couldn't find one in my field. I'm lucky to have my library position."

"If you had a normal schedule we could see more of each other."

"You have a pretty strange schedule."

"But that's to be expected in my profession."

"Well, I have a profession too. I'm a teacher who has to work library hours."

"But it's only part-time—"

"And I'll continue to work there until I find a better position in my profession!" she exclaimed, distraught at her own rising tone.

Rafe stared as though he didn't understand. What did he want? she wondered. Was she supposed to be at his beck and call? Before giving him the chance to say something else that was offensive, she decided to change the subject back to the topic that mattered to *her*. "By the way, what do you plan to do for Christmas?"

"Christmas?"

"This coming Wednesday."

"I don't know. I usually plan Christmas around the kids, but they'll be out of town. Louise is spending the day with her boyfriend and his family. I didn't make plans."

"Okay. Never mind." With a sinking feeling, Melissa realized Rafe hadn't planned anything for Christmas with her at all. It looked like she was going to spend the holiday alone, after all. Hiding her disappointment and anger, she stared down at the table.

"Melissa," Rafe said, lifting her chin and making her look at him. "Are you upset? I hardly know if I'm making sense. I'm so tired, my brains feel like mush." He delicately kissed the tip of her nose. "I didn't make any *specific* plans, but I assumed we'd spend the holiday together."

She smiled at the tickling sensation and at the relief she felt at his words. Letting the tension drain from her, she asked, "How about an invitation from *me?* Could you help me pick out a tree on Monday morning?"

"Of course I can. But how about doing it sooner? Like tomorrow night, after you get home from work?"

"And will you decorate it with me on Christmas Eve?"

"Whatever you want."

Melissa knew what she wanted all right—Rafe. Sharing Christmas with him would make the holiday doubly wonderful. As they kissed she relished the delicious sensation of his warm lips and pressed herself against him.

Rafe paused to catch his breath when he reached the fifth-floor landing. Looking up, he expected to see Melissa at the top of the stairs waiting for him and was surprised when she wasn't there. She'd had enough time to come out of her apartment since he'd buzzed her five flights ago. Maybe she'd grown impatient and gone back inside.

God, he hated all these stairs. They were one of the reasons he didn't come here often. And then there was the fact that he felt uncomfortable in her odd little apartment; it was difficult to feel at home when he had a hard time finding a solid place to sit.

As soon as he felt more rested, Rafe climbed the last flight. Luckily, his headache was better now. He must have taken a a half-dozen aspirin already. All the problems with his kids this morning combined with the anxiety of parting with them had made him doubly jittery.

"Rafe!" Melissa opened the door suddenly, her blue eyes glowing. She was a vision in gold and white, wearing a cream-colored, full-skirted dress with a gold metallic belt and a gold necklace made of strands of tiny bells.

"Ready to go pick out your tree?" He took her in his arms and kissed her thoroughly. "I'm sorry I'm late."

Her pink lips parted enticingly. "Your change in schedule worked to my advantage. The couple of extra hours gave me time to make some refreshments." He reluctantly released her so she could show him a tray of star- and tree-shaped cookies. "Christmas cookies!" she announced with childlike excitement. "We can have a snack before we leave. Would you like tea or coffee?"

"Coffee, thanks."

"I'll make some." She gave him an inquiring look. "Is everything all right? Did Gretta and Hank make their flight?"

"Yeah. We had a difficult time with them, though. They were fighting all the way to the airport. Tension, I suppose. Louise and I both had to threaten them before they'd settle down. Then Gretta started to cry and carry on before she got on the plane because I wasn't going with her."

"I'm sure she recovered once the plane left the ground."

"I hope so, or else the flight attendants were driven

crazy. Nicole didn't bother to tell me how the trip was. And I waited so long for her call telling me they'd arrived safely, I forgot to ask."

"Couldn't you call her?"

"I did, but no one was home. They must have had a long lunch before they got back to her apartment. Who knows? She knew I was waiting, but . . ." He shrugged. He could always count on Nicole to do something irresponsible, but why not get his mind off her and his kids for now? It wasn't fair to burden Melissa with complaints. "Want me to help you make the coffee?" Encircling her waist with an arm, he blew a kiss into her soft cloud of hair.

"There's room for only one cook in this tiny kitchen."

"Even if one of the cooks is tiny?"

She gave him a sweet smile. "Why don't you go in the living room? I'll bring the coffee in a minute. Here." Placing the cookies on an antique china plate, she handed it to him. "Don't eat them all before I get there."

Rafe walked through the two small rooms that led to the larger one. Lighted candles burned tonight instead of lamps, and in the semidarkness he stumbled and almost fell onto her futon mattress laying on the floor. Several cookies slid off the plate and Rafe cursed as he stooped to pick them up. Melissa ought to invest in some normal furniture one of these days.

He picked his way to the card table, where he put down the plate. Feeling around for the switch of an overhead Japanese lantern, he managed to turn the light on and then sat down in the wooden rocker and looked around. To one side was a fragile-looking rattan love seat. Although it was painted nicely and covered with flowery cushions, Rafe was sure he could lift the thing with one hand and had doubts about it being able to support his weight. On the other side of the table was a director's chair with a sagging canvas seat that looked like it would rip if anyone sat in it.

Shaking his head, Rafe leaned over the rickety table to

take a couple of cookies. The Sunday paper was spread out on top of the table, open to the employment ads. He noticed a few were circled, and as he examined them his eyebrows rose.

"What's this? 'Waitress wanted for roller-skating restaurant. Part-time. Must be able to work evenings and weekends,'" he read aloud. "And this one? 'Volunteer for psychological experiments at university. Paid by the hour.'"

Humming, Melissa carried a tray with the coffee and cups into the room. To add a holiday touch she'd placed a couple of Christmas decorations on the tray as well, one of them a tiny, haloed angel. She thought Rafe was talking to himself until she caught the gist of his words.

"Are you really considering being a costumed representative of the Hot-Cha-Cha Popcorn Company?" he asked incredulously. "And passing out samples in supermarkets?"

Melissa colored as she set down the coffee. "I was just looking. I need another job, you know. The Santa's helper position will be over this Tuesday."

"Some of these jobs are for weekends or evenings."

"Well, I have to take what I can get, seeing as I need to work it around my library hours." Was he going to start criticizing her work situation again? Melissa wondered. Wanting to fully celebrate the season, she'd like to forget her problems at the moment. Grim reality would set in soon enough when she'd start needing money by this time next week. "Let's put the paper away." She tried to fold it up.

"Just a minute." He pointed to another circled ad. "What about this one? 'Environmentalist wanted. Get paid for demonstrating against toxic waste.'"

"I marked jobs I thought looked interesting. I planned to eliminate some of them when I read them more closely." Her face grew warmer with embarrassment. She hadn't meant to share her frustrating job search with Rafe.

"You could eliminate all of these. They certainly won't pay much. These aren't jobs for an adult."

How could he start a fight now? Melissa wondered angrily, stubbornly setting her jaw. "Are you insinuating I'm not mature?"

"I didn't say that. But look at all this." He gestured at the room. "You could afford real furniture if you got a full-time job. You have to admit you're not living like a person should at your age."

"According to whose standards?"

"Melissa." Rafe's voice was placating as he rose from the rocker to approach her, but she stiffened and stepped away. "Be realistic. If you can't find a full-time teaching job, do what you can with your education. There are other fields. Sometimes we have to compromise. Can you type?"

"No. Can you?" Hurt and insulted, struggling to hold back tears, Melissa headed for the kitchen. Lately she'd had a hard time feeling successful anyway. He didn't have to make her feel worse.

Rafe followed her, but when he tried to touch her, she whirled on him.

"I'm doing the best I can, Rafe. I've told you that before. And I happen to love my library job."

"Are you sure you don't love the freedom you have . . . from responsibility?"

"I am responsible!" she cried. "I'd be happy to have a full-time position."

"Are you sure you don't enjoy taking these goofy jobs? Never knowing what surprises might come up next?"

Melissa glared at him furiously. "My 'goofy jobs' are none of your damn business!"

He scowled. "They ought to be somebody's business. I realize your family's not here to—"

"My family?" she sputtered. "What are you trying to do —play daddy? I have one father, Rafe Damon. I certainly don't need a second one."

"Your father?" He reddened and his dark eyes snapped. "Now *that* was a childish statement. I'm only trying to give you good advice!"

"Well, I don't appreciate your advice!" she cried as they stood glowering at each other.

"Fine. Maybe you don't appreciate *me*, either. Maybe I should leave."

"Why don't you?"

Before he could say anything else, she took his coat from the nearby counter and shoved it at him. Turning on his heel, he slammed out the door, making its wooden panels reverberate behind him.

Melissa jumped when the loose rod of the police lock crashed to the floor, barely missing her foot. Cursing as she put the lock back together, she managed to choke out, "And Merry Christmas to you, too, Rafe Damon!"

CHAPTER SIX

"Santa, you better be good tonight. None of that foolin' around like you used to do before the pink sugarplum fairy here straightened you out," Arlene said, jerking a thumb in Melissa's direction. "You got some serious work to do after midnight."

"Your admonishment strikes me to the quick, Arlene. I'm a reformed man, remember? Now if *you're* good, you might get what you want for Christmas. Ho-ho-ho!"

Arlene smacked Clarence's pillowed paunch affectionately before heading for the women's dressing room. "I'm always good! Ask my boyfriend, Bill," she saucily added. "He'll make sure I get what I want! Merry Christmas, now."

"Merry Christmas!" When Clarence turned to Melissa, his expression sobered. "I'm sorry to say I can't think of a thing that will help make your Christmas wishes come true, my girl. Finding a full-time teaching job can be a problem, but I did so hope the thing with Rafe would fulfill one of your requests."

Melissa remembered making the wishes for romance and financial stability which Clarence jokingly had granted her after she'd helped save his job.

"But Terry's told me that hardheaded photographer still hasn't called and begged your forgiveness," he grumbled.

Wishing Terry hadn't said anything to Clarence about her disagreement with Rafe, Melissa smiled bravely while trying to block a pair of dark bedroom eyes from her memory. "Oh, it'll all work out for the best."

When Clarence frowned down at her, she knew she hadn't fooled him. "Nevertheless, I happen to have a small thank-you tucked away in my pocket." He pulled out a tiny package. "Something to remind you of your naughty Santa."

"Oh, Clarence, I'd never forget you!" Melissa opened the green and red wrapping and revealed a miniature pink fairy on a gold cord. "Oh!"

"An ornament for your tree."

"It's beautiful. Thank you." Melissa hugged the older man and quickly released him. "I've got to change."

"Of course. Merry Christmas, Melissa."

"You, too, Clarence."

She couldn't make herself say the words "Merry Christmas" any more than she could admit she had no tree on which to hang the beautiful little ornament. She couldn't say Rafe had promised to help her pick one out and get it up to her apartment Sunday evening, nor that they'd planned to decorate it on Christmas Eve, tonight, but they'd fought instead and now Melissa didn't have the heart to buy a tree, let alone trim it by herself.

Trying to swallow the lump that had been lodged in her throat since Sunday night, Melissa entered the dressing room and changed into her street clothes while trying to ignore the growing air of festivity around her. Christmas was here, impossible to ignore no matter how hard she tried. Christmas carols were piped throughout the store, and cheerful holiday greetings echoed off the metal lockers.

"You'd better hurry, girl. There's hardly more than an hour left to finish your Christmas shopping!"

Arlene's excited words cut through her thoughts and Melissa realized she'd been staring blindly at her sparkling pink costume. "Oh, you're right," she said, not wanting to admit that she had nothing to purchase. "I was just thinking about how much I was going to miss everyone. Especially you."

"Hey, now don't get all sentimental on me. I live in uptown Manhattan, not upstate New York."

"Right."

Quickly, Melissa hung up the dress, carefully folded the wings, then encased it in a protective plastic covering. She wished she could leave the costume behind—one less reminder of the holiday she wouldn't be celebrating, one less reminder of Rafe and how she'd met him pretending to be the tooth fairy. But that would be foolish, a waste of the hard-earned money she'd paid for it.

Perhaps she could sell it to one of the secondhand clothing shops she enjoyed poking through. She could use the money. But remembering Rafe's first kiss, the way he'd crushed her wings, and the way her rhinestone tiara had spilled onto his darkly handsome brow, Melissa knew she'd never part with the costume.

"Merry Christmas, girl." Arlene hugged Melissa and headed for the door with a warning. "Don't eat too many sugarplums tonight!"

Melissa had to grin at the other woman's teasing. "Don't worry, I won't." Actually, she wasn't sure *what* she was going to eat that night. "And call me like you promised."

"I'll call."

Melissa hoped Arlene would. It was much more difficult to make friends in a big city like New York than it was in her small hometown. She'd miss the black woman's sense of humor and high spirits, which never seemed to flag. Right now she could use large doses of both positive qualities herself. Gathering her things, she said her last goodbyes to the other women she'd worked with before leaving the dressing room.

Her brows drawn, her mouth tense, Melissa struggled through the still-crowded store. Just before she reached the revolving doors she was surprised to hear the familiar voice of her boss, Huxley Benton.

"Hmm. I can tell you're not in a party mood tonight."

"Is it that obvious?" Melissa asked, pausing next to the cosmetics counter where he stood.

"I'm afraid so. But I have to admit it's nice to see someone without a big dose of disgusting Christmas cheer written all over them. These holidays wear me out."

Glancing at the wry expression on his handsome face, Melissa wondered if Hux was really as cynical as he seemed to be—or had he raised a defensive shield because he, too, was spending the holiday alone? She wasn't about to ask. Instead, she took the opportunity to broach the topic of future employment.

"Say, Hux, remember those test shots you wanted?"

"How could I forget? They were terrific. You really have some kind of magic, kid. I've presented a few new promotion ideas to the other execs. Don't worry, I have you in mind. Budgeting decisions will be made in a few weeks, after all this holiday folderol is over. I promise I'll let you know the minute the idea's approved."

"No problem." Backing away toward the door, Melissa smiled to hide her disappointment that the news was not more definite. "You've got my number. It's best if you call me mornings."

"Right. Or I'll pass the message through Rafe. By the way, you two have a good one."

Wondering if she should tell Hux she and Rafe wouldn't be spending the holiday together, she realized he was already distracted by a willowy redhead inspecting the cosmetics counter. He murmured something about taking her to a wild party after the store closed. Perhaps she'd been correct about Hux's having no one with whom to spend the holiday. Melissa quickly headed out of Haldan-Northrop and onto Fifth Avenue.

Even though it was scarcely an hour before the stores

closed, people were busy with last-minute Christmas shopping. Arms loaded high with packages, they hurried down the street and jostled each other for space on overcrowded busses. One pedestrian ran into her, almost knocking her over while rushing to the curb to flag down an empty taxi. The woman didn't even stop to see if Melissa was all right.

Melissa thought of her own family and home. Were the Pennsylvania mountains already blanketed with snow? Manhattan had been overcast all day, gloomy with the threat of snow which had not yet fallen. Would New York have a white Christmas? All that remained of the previous week's snowfall were dwindling piles scattered here and there, heavily encrusted with the gray soot of the city.

Melissa couldn't help it if her thoughts were equally gray: she needed a job, but more than that, she needed Rafe.

The subway ride was more boisterous than usual. Ignoring the good cheer, Melissa quietly kept to herself, banishing thoughts of Rafe and thinking instead of her family. She wondered if her parents and brothers had received the package of presents she'd sent more than a week ago. Maybe she'd call them when she got home. That might help pick up her spirits.

But upon entering the vestibule of her building she had yet another disappointment awaiting her, a letter from her ex-roommate, who still had title to the lease on the apartment.

Melissa read the letter as she climbed the six flights of stairs. By the time she got to her landing she was fighting tears. Returning to New York in the spring, Julie and her husband planned to move into the apartment. Melissa would understand. And since she had until April 1, there'd be no problem with her finding another apartment for herself, right?

A few straggling tears rolled down Melissa's cheeks as she unlocked her door and turned on the kitchen light.

Dragging her feet over the worn linoleum, she made her way to the bedroom and hung up her costume, after which she found a box of tissues, then sniffled and blew her way into the front room.

The only reason she could afford *this* apartment was because it was still rent controlled. Another place in the neighborhood would rent for three or four times the amount. And since she hadn't found other work to replace her job at Haldan-Northrop, she now earned only the modest income from the reading program.

Dropping her jacket on the floor, Melissa picked up the wrapped present she'd bought for Rafe and hugged it to her chest. Still in the dark, she sank into her rocking chair and stared out the window, allowing the collected misery of the past few days free reign. She sobbed out loud. Melissa had thought she'd been miserable last Christmas when she'd had the flu and had to remain huddled under her electric blanket after the furnace conked out, but this was going to be the worst Christmas ever!

No secure job.

No apartment.

No Rafe.

What was she going to do?

Heaving a large sigh and wiping her eyes with a tissue, Melissa stared out into the night at the Empire State Building. For years it had been the tallest building in the world, the beacon of the city of dreams. What had happened to her dreams? Melissa wondered. As if to taunt her, the view from her sixth-floor apartment subtly changed as the lights of the Art Deco tower were veiled by a translucent curtain and she realized it was going to be a white Christmas after all.

Mesmerized by the large white flakes, Melissa remembered the first time Rafe had climbed the six flights to her apartment. It had snowed that night too. He'd kissed her and she'd imagined them drifting high above the city, gliding through the night sky like snowflakes—

A loud banging noise from the kitchen startled her. Someone was at the door, obviously determined to get in. Who could it be?

"Rafe?" Her heart beating with excitement, Melissa scrambled to her feet while wiping her eyes. Had Rafe really decided to patch things up? Would this be a wonderful Christmas after all? Still clutching his present, she raced through the dark to the kitchen, already counting the hours they would share together and imagining the ways they would make up for their harsh words to each other. At the repeated knock she yelled, "I'm coming!" But, about to open the door, her big-city caution made Melissa pause before releasing the lock. "Who's there?"

"Why, it's Santa Claus and his favorite elf, my girl. Ho ho ho! Merry Christmas!"

It wasn't Rafe. Hoping they wouldn't read the disappointment on her face, Melissa opened the door for her friends. Her eyes grew wide—they were both still in costume. Had they taken the subway home dressed like that?

"Merry Christmas, Melissa." Terry looked at the package she was still holding. "A present for me?"

Melissa jiggled Rafe's present nervously and set it down on the boards over the bathtub. "I—I thought you were someone else."

"We weren't sure if you had plans, so we decided to invite you to dinner," Terry said, pointing to the larger of the two paper bags Clarence held. "It's Chinese. We even got turkey fried rice to celebrate the season."

"Thanks, but I don't think—"

"Having a pretty female dinner companion would certainly cheer up a poor old overworked Santa," Clarence grumbled, then checked her reaction from beneath his white brows.

94

"And Santa doesn't look like he's the only one who needs cheering up," Terry added.

Knowing they couldn't miss her red nose or swollen eyes, Melissa responded with a quivering smile. "You're both sweet, but I wouldn't want to ruin your holiday."

"Nonsense, my girl, nonsense. Now, are you going to let us in before this food gets cold?"

Hesitating only a second—for even in her misery, Melissa didn't want to be alone—she agreed. "Maybe we can make our own Christmas cheer."

"Smashing idea. I have all the ingredients." Clarence set the bags down and emptied the smaller one, pulling out red wine, aquavit, an orange, a lemon, cinnamon sticks, and other spices. "The secret for magical glogg has been passed down through my family for generations."

Clarence went to work preparing the glogg while Melissa and Terry set the card table in the front room.

"Where's your Christmas tree?" Terry asked.

"Rafe was going to help me pick one out. I got the ornaments out and everything," Melissa said, pointing to a box.

She made a centerpiece by crowding together a dozen candles of varying sizes. When she lit them and the others on the shelves, the room glowed cozily. Then Terry tuned into a radio station playing Christmas music.

"Appropriately festive," Clarence declared, sauntering in from the kitchen. "But aren't you going to change?"

Realizing he meant her, Melissa asked, "Into what?"

"Into a sugarplum fairy. Would our Christmas celebration be complete with only a Santa and one elf?"

Knowing protesting would be useless, Melissa hurried and donned her costume along with a smile. How could she remain sad with two caring friends to gladden her heart?

When she came back into the front room her smile widened. Clarence and Terry were decorating her potted palm like a Christmas tree. They'd strung it with twinkling white lights and now were adding ornaments. Melissa hung the tiny fairy Clarence had given her near the top of the tree. She tried not to imagine what the evening would have been like if Rafe had been helping her decorate the Scotch pine she'd wanted.

Under her friends' crazy influence, Melissa managed to have a better time than she would have thought possible. Only occasionally did Rafe Damon creep back into her thoughts to steal her laughter. After they ate their barely warm Chinese food, Clarence poured the glogg.

"Are you sure it won't dissolve my insides?" Melissa asked hoarsely after taking her first sip.

"On the contrary. Be assured it will keep you healthy. Germs don't stand a chance against this stuff."

The glogg left a heated trail down to her stomach. Even so, the effects of the powerful drink snuck up on Melissa. "The room is spinning and I'm not even dancing."

"What you need is fresh air," Clarence said at the same time he poured another round. "Let's go Christmas caroling."

"On the streets of New York? You're crazy!"

"Oh, come on, Melissa," Terry urged. "It will be fun!"

"But it's snowing!"

"Merely atmosphere to set the stage, my girl."

Giggling, she headed for her bedroom. "All right, but I guess I'd better dress warmer." Donning white woolen tights and a turtleneck under her costume, Melissa wondered whether she was going along with their scheme because she was drunk or just plain crazy. Well, maybe caroling would help keep her mind off her problems. Grabbing a velvet cape she'd bought in a secondhand clothing store, Melissa rejoined her friends. "I'm ready."

"No you're not," Terry countered, holding up a sprig of green. "You've got to wear my magical Christmas present."

"Mistletoe?"

"Don't you know about mistletoe magic? When you're standing under it you become irresistible." He pinned the sprig in her golden tresses, then kissed her on the cheek. "See what I mean?"

Melissa laughed. "Let's go. I get to be in the middle so you two can hold me up. Boy, that glogg is strong stuff!"

Afterward, Melissa wondered how she made it down the six flights of steps, even with help. Once outside, Clarence navigated them along the streets of Manhattan, heading south in the general direction of Greenwich Village.

In a matter of hours the gray city had magically turned into a sparkling winter wonderland. Letting the fresh setting inspire her imagination, Melissa easily got into the spirit of the holiday. The trio melodically haunted the snow-covered streets, singing loudly if slightly off key, stopping whenever people greeted them merrily. Melissa was surprised when a few people offered them money after listening to their rendition of "Jingle Bells," appalled when Clarence took off his hat and collected it.

"Do you think it's right to take people's money on Christmas Eve?" Melissa protested.

"A small compensation for being out of work," Clarence said, transferring the money to a pocket. "They obviously don't need it or they wouldn't have offered, and it might buy the three of us a good meal when we need it."

It was difficult to argue with Clarence's logic.

"Hey, Santa, I gotta ask for something I forgot, okay?" called a towheaded boy from his second-story window.

"Yes, my lad? What is it?" Clarence boomed in his official Santa voice.

"Do you think you could make my mom have a boy this time? I already got two sisters. Mom's in the hospital right now!"

"Well, I'm going to be awfully busy tonight, so I can't promise, but I shall see what I can do."

"Thanks, Santa!"

All three stifled their laughter as they went on, this time singing "Have Yourself a Merry Little Christmas." Wasn't

97

that what she was doing? Melissa thought, irritated when a couple kissing under a streetlight made her think of Rafe.

Why couldn't she forget the dratted man? He hadn't exactly been eager to include her in his holiday plans to begin with, Melissa thought, forcing herself to remember how he'd excluded her from sharing the pleasure of trimming his tree with the kids. Then, because he'd been upset about them going to visit Nicole, he'd picked a fight with her, criticizing her life-style. To top it off, he hadn't called either to apologize or to say he wasn't coming over tonight.

Having no doubts that Rafe Damon was off somewhere having a good time—maybe at the same party as Hux—Melissa was determined to have as merry a Christmas as he!

"Rafe, dear, you can't sit here in the dark by yourself all night. Not on Christmas Eve."

"I'm not sitting in the dark. The Christmas-tree lights are on and I've got a fire going. Would you feel better if I turned on all the lights in the living room?"

"That's not what I meant, and you know it. I've got an idea. Why don't you get dressed up and come to the party with us? Charles is due any minute, but I'm sure he wouldn't mind waiting for you."

"Good Lord, Louise, don't you think I'd feel ridiculous tagging along with my mother and her date?"

"You could have your own date if you'd stop being so stubborn and call Melissa. I don't know what you two fought about, but I'm sure you could resolve it if you wanted to, especially considering the holiday. Haven't you ever heard of peace on earth and goodwill to men? That means kiss and make up."

"The holidays don't have anything to do with anything," Rafe grumbled, staring out the window at the falling snow.

"Really? Isn't that why you're so out of sorts?" Louise

asked carefully. "Because the children have gone off to visit with Nicole for the holidays?"

"Maybe, but I can't help it, Louise. I know Nicole is going to do something irresponsible to disappoint Gretta and Hank again."

"You don't know that." Though her words were meant to be reassuring, her tone was worried.

"I feel it. Every time they visit her they come back mixed up and unhappy and then you and I have to deal with the problem. What can I do? I can't keep them from her. No matter how thoughtless or self-centered she is, Nicole is still their mother and they love her. I just wish she'd grow up."

"And I wish you wouldn't take out your anxieties on Melissa. You know she was expecting to spend the evening with you." Louise gave her son a significant stare and sighed dramatically. "Poor little thing. I can just imagine how deserted she feels, all alone on Christmas Eve. Why, Melissa is probably sitting in front of her window watching the snowflakes fall—forlornly waiting for a certain stubborn son of mine to call to apologize."

"Louise, I'd appreciate it if you let me live my own life. I may be your son, but I'm not your little boy," Rafe growled. Nor was he Melissa's father! he silently added for good measure, still rankling at her heated remark.

"Pardon me. I didn't mean to interfere." Louise's dark eyes expressed anything but an apology. "Don't worry about it. From now on if you want to be an ass, Rafe dear, go right ahead. I certainly won't try to stop you."

With that she stiffly marched down the steps to her own quarters, leaving Rafe feeling guilty as hell. Was he going to spoil *everyone's* holiday? he wondered. Bad enough he'd ruined his own by picking that fight with Melissa about her work. All he'd wanted was to spend more time with her, and now he had none at all.

Maybe he should call her. He had promised to help trim

her Christmas tree. On the other hand, he wasn't sure she had one since he'd also promised to help pick one out. After thinking about it Rafe decided calling Melissa would be the right thing to do. And if she *had* bought a tree, perhaps she'd still want his help decorating it.

With unaccustomed excitement, Rafe dialed her number. He let the phone ring an interminable number of times, but there was no answer. She wasn't home. Sadly, he hung up. It hadn't taken Melissa long to find someone else with whom to spend Christmas Eve. Was it with a new man or an old acquaintance, someone she used to date before she met him?

Popping out of his chair, Rafe paced the floor, tripping over the coffee table in the dark. Damn, but he was clumsy in addition to being irritable and restless. Maybe he *should* go to the party. Hux would probably show. But as he thought it he heard the downstairs door open. Gravitating to the window, he saw Charles help Louise into his Mercedes.

Did everyone have someone with whom they could share their Christmas Eve except him?

After stoking the fire and adding another log, Rafe stooped next to the tree and found the present he'd bought Melissa. He sat down and gently touched the wrapping as though it were her skin. Would he ever see her in the filigreed gold earrings set with sapphires he'd found in an antique shop? She'd look beautiful in them. She'd look beautiful in anything—or nothing at all.

He had to stop that or he'd drive himself crazy.

Rafe told himself that Melissa Ryan was *not* the right woman for him. He was mature and loaded with responsibilities, carefully looking to the future. Melissa lived from day to day. They just weren't right for each other.

He was already crazy if he believed that.

No matter how hard he tried, Rafe couldn't stop thinking about the woman who'd become so important to him in such a short time. Staring into the flames, he replayed scenes from their relationship, imagining Melissa in all her moods. Eventually he grew drowsy, and time slipped away.

"Why don't you give a little love on Christmas Day . . ."

Rafe woke with a start, trying to focus on the faint but melodic words. Someone was singing out front. Checking his watch, he realized it was just about midnight.

Who in the world was out there at this time of night singing Christmas carols? Rafe yawned loudly and rose, intending to check it out. A soft clunk at his foot made him pause. Picking up the object, he realized it was Melissa's present. After setting it down carefully on the coffee table, he headed for the window.

Peering down through the moving curtain of snowflakes to the crystal-coated street, he noticed a small group of people, one of them a rotund man in red. Santa Claus? Rafe rubbed the sleep from his eyes and looked again, but the apparition didn't disappear. Someone must be ready to deliver presents to a bunch of kids or something. Well, it was late, so instead of worrying about it, he was going to bed. His hand closing over the blind lever, he noted the shorter man next to Santa. Didn't the green elf look familiar?

Shrugging, about to close the blinds, Rafe hesitated when he spotted a sparkly pink dress. It couldn't be. He pressed his nose right up against the glass and squinted hard. But it was!

How did they end up on Rafe's street? Melissa wondered, staring at the brownstone's darkened windows. Had fate guided her here, of all places? Or could she thank a matchmaking Santa and elf? Clarence and Terry were both trying very hard to appear innocent as they began "Give Love on Christmas Day." Smiling happily at the song's message, Melissa sang her heart out.

How appropriate! When they finished the song she'd rush right across the street to wish Rafe a merry Christmas! So what if they'd had some stupid argument? It didn't mean they didn't care about each other. He'd been too tense about his kids' departure. Perhaps she'd been too sensitive because she'd been worried about money. Were those good enough reasons to keep them apart? Melissa didn't think so. And since someone had to make the first move, why shouldn't she play the good fairy one more time?

Twirling with joy, Melissa spotted Rafe, his nose pressed against the window. She waved wildly, but slightly dizzy from whirling around, bumped into a large man who momentarily blocked her view. By the time she untangled herself from the stranger, Rafe was no longer in the window.

Melissa's throat went dry and the note she was singing went sour, then died. Hot tears sprang to her eyes and her newfound merriment dissolved like melted snow.

Rafe hadn't wanted to acknowledge her.

Her eyes met those of her friends. Sensing her distress, they, too, stopped singing. Dejectedly, she backed away, planning to find a quick way home as nearby church bells toned the hour.

It was midnight.

CHAPTER SEVEN

Rafe practically tripped down the stairs in his eagerness to get to Melissa. She'd come to make up, to spend what was left of Christmas Eve with him. They would be together after all! As he sped down the hallway he strained to hear the cheerful caroling voices, but the only sounds he could discern were church bells. Why weren't Melissa and her friends still singing?

Eagerly throwing open the door—hoping to see Melissa on his stoop or at least heading for it—Rafe yelled, "Merry Christmas!" into the snowy night, then froze as he realized the small crowd across the street had drifted off. Melissa herself was walking away, her head hung dejectedly, followed by Santa and his elf. "Wait!" He rushed out of the doorway at a frantic pace, unmindful of the snow beneath his feet. His "Melissa, don't leave!" was just as frantic as he went down hard when his feet slipped out from under him. "Damn!"

But he was up in a shot, slipping and sliding across the sidewalk, then across the street to a wide-eyed Melissa, who'd turned to witness his almost acrobatic progress.

"Rafe!"

"Merry Christmas, my very own sugarplum fairy." He spoke softly, his words punctuated by the vaporized cloud formed by his heaving breath. His chest hurt as he studied her by the light of the streetlight and the sparkling snow. He tried to discern her expression. Wasn't she glad to see him? Why had she been leaving? He touched her soft curls as he asked, "And just where did you think you were going?"

Her lips curled into a slow smile, and her cheek dimpled beguilingly, making his breath catch in his throat. Rafe lost control. Joyfully lifting Melissa in his arms, he twirled her so fast that her pink tulle skirts billowed wildly around them and she had to clasp her rhinestone tiara in place so that it wouldn't fly off.

"Merry Christmas, everyone!" he shouted just before they both went down into the snow, laughing happily.

"Merry Christmas, Rafe."

Tenderly he kissed the lips that spoke his name so intimately, shutting out the world around them. She was so very soft and lovable, Rafe thought.

"Merry Christmas, kids," Terry said, gleefully interrupting what should have been a private moment.

"Should I assume I have you two to thank for this very special delivery?" Rafe asked Clarence and Terry as he got up, lifted Melissa from the ground, then brushing the snow from her dress and cape.

"No thanks needed, my good man. Just see that you treat her with all due respect."

"Don't worry. I will." Rafe pulled Melissa close to his heart and hugged her fiercely. "But tell me, how could you be sure I'd be home? I could have gone to a party or something, and then your matchmaking would have been in vain."

"That thought did occur to me, but I decided if you cared about Melissa, you'd be sitting home alone, just as miserable as she was."

"Clarence!" Melissa's exclamation was followed by a reluctant shrug and a happy smile. "I've never been set up so wonderfully."

Clarence nodded regally. "I always attempt to pay my debts in full."

Melissa pulled out of Rafe's arms to hug him, then Terry. "Thank you both."

"It's cold out here," Rafe said, realizing his teeth were beginning to chatter. "Let's go inside and finish our conversation in front of a nice warm fire. I can heat up some glogg."

"Oh, no!" Melissa wailed. "Now *he* wants me to drink that poisonous stuff!"

Terry grinned. "Don't defame Clarence's brew. After all, it worked. Now you two go on and have a good time."

"We have other stops to make," Clarence added.

"If you're sure?" Rafe shivered as melted snow began to seep through his clothing. "Well, Merry Christmas, then. And thanks again."

As they headed for the brownstone, Rafe heard Santa boom, "Merry Christmas to all, and to all a good night!"

"I'll drink to that!" Rafe said, putting an arm around Melissa and hugging her tightly to his side.

"As long as it's not with glogg," Melissa muttered. "My head's going to be too big for my tiara in the morning."

Rafe swept her into the entryway and closed the door, then trapped her against it. Touching her face, he whispered, "I can't believe you're really here."

Kissing her gently, he was thrilled when Melissa pressed her body into his and snaked her arms up around his neck. Rafe groaned and kissed her more deeply, exploring all the warm, secret crevices of her mouth with his tongue. His body instantly responded to the intimate search. He'd always thought he was a patient man, but he couldn't wait to possess her. He wanted Melissa so much, he imagined the melted snow on their clothing was sizzling into clouds of steam around them.

Melissa broke the kiss. "You're shaking with cold. We'd better get to that fireplace before you get sick."

"I'm not shaking because I'm cold," he muttered, but

didn't protest when she wiggled out of his arms and tugged him toward the stairs with a silvery laugh.

Once upstairs, Rafe put another log on the fire while Melissa spread her damp cape over a chair and pulled it close to the fireplace. The flames glinted off the fake stones of her tiara, made her golden hair gleam, and brought a becoming flush to her porcelain skin. How could he have tried to convince himself she wasn't right for him? She was beautiful. She was caring. She was perfect.

Intent on watching her rather than concentrating on what he was doing, Rafe almost burned himself when she turned to him and innocently asked, "Aren't you going to get out of those wet clothes?"

Exactly what he longed to do, Rafe thought, but he was determined to woo Melissa romantically, not frighten her by stripping right there. He was sure she meant for him to change into other clothes in his bedroom, and he had no intention of leaving her alone for a minute. They'd wasted too much time already.

"Why don't you sprinkle some of your fairy dust on me?" he suggested with a grin. "That'll keep me from catching cold."

"At least take off that turtleneck," she insisted, moving next to him and kneeling. Melissa grabbed the bottom of the sweater and pulled it up determinedly. Forcing him to lift his arms, she tugged it over his head. "There, doesn't that feel better?"

"Uh, yeah," Rafe said in a strangled voice.

"Did the wet snow soak all the way through?" She proceeded to check, running her fingers over his arms, stroking his chest and back through the red T-shirt he still wore. "Hmm. Your T-shirt is kind of damp. Maybe you should take it off too."

She was going to drive him crazy. "No!" Rafe exclaimed, staying her hands. If she wasn't careful that pretty little fairy was going to find herself minus a pair of wings! "I'm fine. Really."

"Oh." Melissa settled down facing him, her back to the tree, its twinkling lights outlining her fragile form. Her brows drew together in a frown. "I was just trying to help."

"Thanks," Rafe muttered gruffly, turning to the fireplace, trying to cool the fire inside him. Picking up a poker, he prodded the logs until the flames crackled and danced. "I didn't mean to shout."

Could he make love to her now, after they'd fought? Rafe wondered. Melissa was special and he hadn't wanted to chase her away by moving too fast, as he'd done when he'd backed her into the closet. Trying to dispel her initial impression of him, he'd taken it slow. And since they both had crazy work schedules and he had two kids underfoot to boot, being romantic hadn't been easy.

But the kids were in California. Neither he nor Melissa had to work in the morning. And the setting was definitely romantic. So what was stopping him? The answer was simple: guilt.

What was he thinking about? Melissa wondered as she watched the firelight flicker over Rafe's changing expressions. Their argument? When he'd picked on her life-style, even criticizing her furniture, she'd been angry and insulted. But looking around at the oversized pieces in his living room, she thought she understood why he'd done so.

Rafe's furniture was solid and comfortable, representative of his life-style. He was merely having trouble understanding hers—he'd never even had to look for a job, working as he had with his father—and she'd overreacted to his comments because she wasn't necessarily living the way she wanted to but the way she'd been forced to by circumstances.

"Melissa, about Sunday night," Rafe said as though he could read her thoughts. "Umm, I wasn't in a top-notch mood."

"I noticed," Melissa said with surprising good humor.

"It was the kids. I was worried about them, but I shouldn't have taken my anxiety out on you," he admitted. "I'm sorry."

"So am I."

He really did look guilty, Melissa thought, noticing the way Rafe's eyes slid away from her. And uncomfortable. But why? Because of his guilt or because he was still trying to control his physical attraction to her? That thought set her pulse racing. Silly man. Hadn't he been aware she'd asked for more than his kisses when she'd removed his sweater?

But before she could tell him as much, Rafe handed her a pink foil package tied with silver ribbons. "This is for you."

Melissa carefully unwrapped it. Her eyes wide, she held up the delicate earrings so their dark blue stones winked in the firelight. Such a special present—one that had required time and care to find—from a very special man. She could tell the gold filigree and sapphire earrings were real antiques. How had Rafe known they'd be the perfect gift? She hadn't thought he'd noticed her penchant for old, romantic clothes and jewelry.

"I've never had anything so beautiful. Thank you." Fastening them, she asked, "Do they go with my pointed ears?"

"I'll have to look closer." Rafe leaned forward, lacing his fingers through her golden curls. "Mmm. Perfectly."

Toes tingling with expectancy, she brushed her mouth against his and thought of the antique photographs of his Greenwich Village neighborhood she'd bought him. "Your present's sitting neglected on my bathtub."

"But Santa brought me a better one."

"It's after midnight. Don't you think you should unwrap it and see what you got?"

"I already know I got the best present Santa's ever delivered."

Melissa sighed in disappointment. Couldn't the man take a hint? Leaning back, she stuck her small foot square in his chest. "You can start with this end." Let him ignore that.

Various emotions flitted over Rafe's face before realization set in. Then his lids drooped enticingly, making his bedroom eyes seem sexier than ever. Thank goodness he finally caught on! Melissa thought as he slowly drew a hand down her calf, leaving exquisite sensations in its wake. After torturing her ankle with his fingertips, he tugged off her ballet slipper.

"Rafe, no!" Melissa yelped as he tickled her foot.

"Isn't this part of my present?" he asked innocently. "Oh, it's wet. I'd better fix that. I wouldn't want it to warp." Rafe covered her foot with both hands and massaged it until Melissa's laughter turned into ecstatic sighs as she leaned back on her elbows. "You never explained about the wings."

"Explained what?" Melissa murmured, reluctant to talk. She didn't want to distract herself from the wonderful waves of pleasure shooting through her. Head hung back, she watched the Christmas-tree lights blink on and off, imagining they pulsated to the same rhythm as the sensual ripplings.

"Do the wings come off first or are they attached? I want to unwrap my gift properly."

"If I told you, that would be cheating."

Rafe sighed with mock exasperation. "Then I guess I'll just have to find out for myself."

With a quick, hard tug on her ankle, he had Melissa flat on her back, snuggling against him. Her rhinestone tiara flew off behind her. He easily flipped her over, ignoring her giggling, halfhearted protests. Her mirth died quickly, however, once Rafe found her costume's zipper and slowly, teasingly undid it. He pulled up the back of the turtleneck she'd donned for warmth, following the movement with the brush of his lips up her spine.

"Oh!"

"My gift has sensual uses, I see," Rafe murmured.

"Really?" Melissa asked as he turned her over on her back, pulling her arms out of her costume while doing so. "Maybe you ought to try it out. Make sure it works properly."

"Some people sure know how to wrap a good thing so it's hard to get at!" Rafe muttered while trying to remove her turtleneck.

When he finally succeeded and ducked his head to taste her breasts, Melissa arched so that he could more fully enjoy his present, but immediately suspected it was she who was getting the most pleasure from the demonstration. Moaning when his teeth caught her sensitive nipple and it tightened into a hard bud, she let her eyes close and her mind open. . . .

Bright dabs of color splashed against the back of her eyelids like the twinkling lights of a Christmas tree. A beautiful golden-haired princess—or was it a fairy?—twirled around, the jewels of her glowing white dress reflecting the sparkling colors. Her slippered feet moved to the strains of a romantic melody only she could hear.

Then a dark prince appeared. Seizing the princess, he kissed her fiercely, holding her as though he'd never let her go. Suddenly he, too, heard the music and whirled her around in a sensual dance. He kissed her again and magic mists rose to shelter them. . . .

Listening to the crackle and hiss of the fire, languidly opening her eyes, Melissa realized she was naked. While she'd been storytelling inside her head, Rafe had removed her costume. Now he was undressing. She watched with pleasure as he stripped without taking his eyes off her. His briefs were red, just like his T-shirt, which he was in the process of removing.

"I'm not sure which of us is more prettily wrapped," she

said. "You're done up in a more appropriate color for Christmas."

"Not for long."

After pulling off his briefs he moved over her, cradling her under his naked body. She inhaled his spicy scent, which mingled with the fragrance of pine and burning hickory. Rafe's flesh seemed to be licked golden by the fire's flames. Wondering if it would be warm, Melissa ran her fingers over his shoulder. His skin was hot to the touch.

"Melissa, my very own sugarplum fairy," Rafe whispered, his mouth turning into a smile.

He kissed her then, his lips moving slowly over hers, resolutely seducing every fiber of her being. He tasted of roasted chestnuts and glogg and everything that was Christmas. His body stroked hers lightly in the same languid rhythm as his mouth, making Melissa dizzy with desire. It definitely was going to be the best holiday ever, she thought dreamily, returning his passionate embrace.

When he pulled away to stare into her face, she huskily whispered, "Mistletoe magic."

"Huh?"

Smiling into his puzzled brown eyes, Melissa touched the sprig of mistletoe still pinned in her hair. "A Christmas gift from a matchmaking elf. He said it would make me irresistible."

"You don't need mistletoe. You're already irresistible."

"Show me."

To her immense satisfaction, he proceeded to do so, kissing her deeply and exploring her trembling body with fervent hands. They delicately skimmed over every curve and valley, leaving in their wake aching trails of flesh that seemed to pulse with the delicious sensations.

Melissa, too, became an eager explorer, reveling in Rafe's moans, which were muffled by her own insistent mouth. She lightly stroked his hard, muscular body and, pulling her mouth from his, nuzzled the juncture of his neck and shoulder.

Arching into her with a moan, Rafe found the center of her woman's passion. Desire coursed through her so intensely it almost frightened Melissa. But she knew there was no reason to be afraid now. Rafe's was the magic that would spirit her away from her worries. How could she fear anything in his arms? Pressing her lower body against his hand, Melissa allowed herself to reenter the enchanted world only he could create for her.

She was spinning and twirling through the rising mists in the arms of her dark prince until she grew light-headed and her body throbbed with excitement.

"Yes, oh yes. Rafe, love me," she whispered, her voice intense with her need, her body opening to him.

He accepted the provocative invitation, carefully slipping his fingers along the moist trail to her heart of desire, stroking her into a sensual haze. Far off in the distance, flashes of crystal beckoned, luring her closer. She slipped her hands down Rafe's taut stomach, finding and guiding him, inviting him to enter the enchanted world with her.

"Definitely irresistible," he murmured, plunging into her with a satisfied groan.

Twining her arms around his neck, her legs around his back, Melissa laughed with pleasure, the silvery tinkle pervading the air with good cheer. Filled with him, she felt complete as never before. He was her fairy tale, her Christmas, her fondest wish come true, she decided, watching his handsome face catch the flickering firelight.

When Rafe moved within her, Melissa's thoughts scattered, turning into tinsel and snowflakes. The flashes of crystal drew inexplicably closer as he brought them to the brink of a chasm. They hovered there for an interminable time, then they were suddenly plunging in a heart-stopping freefall until they landed on a sparkling cloud of fairy dust.

" 'Give love on Christmas . . .' " Rafe sang as he turned another omelet over in the pan, deftly using the beaten egg mixture to cover a filling of cheese and tomatoes. "How about getting that coffee cake out of the refrigerator, my sweet sugarplum?"

"Don't we have enough food already?" Melissa asked.

He looked at the kitchen table, generously spread with danishes, fruit, sausages, and toast. "I'll eat two of these omelets, okay? And go ahead and look for the coffee cake. I'm hungry. How about mixing the orange juice so we can add some champagne to it? Bubbly brew makes any meal romantic." He gave her a meaningful glance along with his slow smile.

She laughed, the happy sound reverberating against the walls like so many tiny Christmas bells. At least that's how her voice sounded to Rafe. And Melissa looked absolutely ravishing as she stood there in his kitchen clad in nothing but his dark blue terry robe and the earrings he'd given her last night. The gaping front of the garment revealed part of one rounded breast while the side slit exposed a pretty leg to mid-thigh. Warmth rose within him, prompting him to say gruffly, "Come here, little fairy."

She backed away from him, laughing. "You're going to burn your omelet!"

"Oh, right." Reluctantly he turned back to his cooking and scooped the omelet onto a plate. By that time Melissa was adding water to the frozen orange juice. She said mischievously, "You should pay attention to your work or you might end up like the elf that got into trouble with Santa Claus."

"What elf?" he asked, setting the plate on the table and heading for the refrigerator to get the champagne.

"Well, it was like this," Melissa began, opening her eyes wide. "Once upon a time, there was a very naughty elf. He always wanted to do what pleased him and he didn't care

113

about anyone else. Instead of making toys for Christmas, he constantly thought about romance."

"What's so bad about that?"

"He fell in love with a beautiful ballerina doll and neglected his job to spend hours trying to cast a spell that would make her come alive. Finally he succeeded in finding the right combination of magical words that turned the doll into a living, breathing woman. And then"—Melissa paused for emphasis as she handed Rafe the orange juice—"the ballerina became totally mad for her elf."

"Sounds wonderful to me."

"But their love affair made him neglect his work even more. He didn't finish his projects on time and he also packaged the wrong toys for the wrong kids for Christmas."

"Aw. Couldn't they understand the circumstances?"

Melissa shook her head seriously, although he thought the corners of her mouth were turning up. "No, the kids couldn't understand it and neither could Santa. He had to fire the elf and what's worse . . ."

"Yes?"

"The ballerina was *insatiable*. At first the elf liked her attentions, but then he began to worry. She wouldn't let him out of her sight! When he ran away to get some rest, she chased him down the road, she tracked him through the forest, and she followed him across the meadow. Finally she tackled him and knocked him down in a field of daisies. The lovely ballerina couldn't get enough of that elf and, boy, was he tired! Would you like to hear the details? About what she made him do?"

"Now, wait just a minute. I thought this was one of your kids' stories. It seems a little racy for eight-year-olds. Are you trying to turn me on? I can't be responsible for what I might do."

Melissa merely smiled. "They rolled around in the flowers and she removed her ballet slippers and her dancing skirt. Then she took off his little green jacket and his little green pants—"

"That's enough!" he cried, interrupting her and putting down the champagne bottle to give chase. Squealing with delight, she ran around the table, Rafe close behind. He caught her in his arms easily, leaning her back over the wooden tabletop, one of his hands finding its way inside the robe to cover a breast.

"Rafe! I'm lying on a plate!" she exclaimed, squirming beneath him. But her nipple pressed invitingly against his palm.

"Good! I've always wanted to have a sugarplum fairy for Christmas brunch." Rafe covered her mouth with a kiss.

"Good heavens! What's going on up here? Oh!" Louise exclaimed, stopping to stare as she came in the door. "Excuse me!"

Melissa tried to pull the front of the robe back together as Rafe discreetly removed his hand. Both were breathing a little heavily as he released his hold and helped her to stand.

"I didn't mean to intrude," Louise apologized, smiling. "I was coming up for breakfast, but I'll make some coffee downstairs."

Feeling embarrassed, Melissa looked hesitantly at Rafe. "We have plenty of food," she offered.

"We certainly do," he agreed, his serious expression changing to a broad grin. "Come on and join us, Louise. We were, um . . . laughing at a joke."

"I can go back down."

"Nonsense," Rafe told his mother, pulling out a chair. "Sit. I've made enough food for ten people. And we've got enough bubbly for a crowd too. Come on and toast the jolly season with champagne and orange juice."

"Well, if you insist."

Soon they were all laughing and talking as they ate. Once over her initial discomfort, Melissa thought Louise seemed to be warmly accepting and was happy the woman said nothing about her unusual attire. If anything, Louise acted genuinely pleased to see her. Was his mother giving her unspoken blessing to their relationship?

"So, did you and Charles have fun at the party last night?" Rafe asked Louise.

"Charles was charming as usual," she told him. "And the party was very amusing. I didn't get home until 4 A.M."

"I wondered why you got up so late today," Rafe teased, neglecting to add that he himself had been up for only an hour. "Was anyone there I know?"

"Oh, yes. Jack and Diane asked about you. Shirley said to give you season's greetings. And, of course, Hux was there parading around with an outrageously thin redhead—probably a model. He was showing everyone how to do some torrid Caribbean dances and wishing them 'Bah humbug.' You know Hux."

"He always likes to be the wild one at a party," Rafe explained to Melissa as he poured her more champagne and orange juice.

"And he enjoys being a professional cynic," said Louise, laughing. "He was telling everyone about the trouble he had with some neighbors in his apartment building this year. It seems Hux put out a 'Bah humbug' sign and decorated it with yellow and purple lights."

"The other tenants didn't like it?" Rafe asked.

"Hardly. They demanded he remove the sign. Hux said he was surprised. His neighbors are never personally concerned with him and they probably wouldn't move a finger if he was being attacked or robbed. Why should they care about his silly sign? It didn't hurt anyone."

"I guess some people are sentimental about holidays," Melissa offered, remembering her theory about Hux. She was sure he acted cynical and repressed his sentimental feelings because he had no one with whom to share a good old-fashioned Christmas. He probably put up the sign to

116

get someone to notice him. Looking at Louise and then back at Rafe, she was happy she had some loving companions with whom to celebrate.

And what fun they could plan for the next few days! Perhaps they might even celebrate all week. As soon as Louise left for her quarters to prepare for dinner with Charles's family, Rafe and Melissa excitedly discussed their plans.

"Tomorrow, let's go to the photography show at the Museum of Modern Art," suggested Rafe, placing an arm around her.

"And out to dinner afterward," Melissa said, leaning toward him.

"And let's go dancing after dinner."

"That would be wonderful."

"We've got to make up for lost time. Ahem." Rafe lowered his lashes sexily. "I hope we don't get arrested. I don't know if I can stop myself from removing your clothes on the dance floor."

Melissa laughed as he nuzzled her chin, his fragrant breath smelling of champagne. "As long as we're together, I'll risk jail."

"And we can still go out of town if you want. I've got a shoot on Friday, but it won't take long. How about driving up the coast like I suggested before? You really *are* on vacation this week, right?"

She could tell he was being careful. She'd been hurt the last time he'd mentioned leaving town—but that had been because he'd seemed so close-minded about her work situation. Pleased Rafe was being sensitive now, she hastened to assure him, "I'm absolutely free."

"Wonderful," he said, drawing her closer.

Then the phone rang. Glancing toward the instrument on the kitchen wall, he grumbled, "Who can that be?" As he rose to answer it, he turned back to Melissa. "Say, what time is it? Two o'clock?" Eyes suddenly alight with expectancy, he reached for the receiver, explaining, "It must be the kids!"

"Hello? Hank? Merry Christmas! How are you doing? . . . Put Gretta on, will you? . . . Huh?" Melissa watched his smiling face grow serious. "Wait a minute . . . slow down. What happened?" Scowling, he asked abruptly, "Is your mother there? I want to talk to her. Don't worry, Hank, everything will be all right."

Although she couldn't hear the other side of the conversation, Melissa gathered that something had gone wrong with the children or their trip. Filled with concern, she hoped neither Gretta nor Hank was hurt.

"Nicole?" Rafe said, pausing as the other person spoke. "It's an emergency? Why? Doesn't your employer have any respect for your family responsibilities?" His dark eyes seemed to snap with anger. "What about the kids' feelings? . . . Well, okay, I guess I understand. What flight will they be on? . . . Put Hank back on, will you? . . . Son, I'll see you and Gretta tomorrow. And don't worry, we'll have fun here anyway. I'll try to get tickets for a show for Friday. And you've got lots of nice presents here, you know."

Were the children actually coming home? And were the tickets for Friday of *this* week? What about the other plans she and Rafe had just been making? Melissa quickly decided to withhold her questions until she knew exactly what was going on. After hanging up Rafe looked so dejected she rose to comfort him.

Holding her loosely against him, he said, "This changes everything. You must have heard—the kids are coming home tomorrow night. There's an emergency with Nicole's sales job and she has to travel for a week. She sounded upset, although I'm always suspicious about her emergencies. Now we won't be able to go to the photography show and we certainly can't go out of town."

"I'll be happy to help you take the kids somewhere," Melissa suggested.

He seemed hesitant. "Thanks, but in circumstances like these, it's better if I deal with them alone. They're very upset. When they get home they'll have to talk it out with me. Let's not make any definite plans for going out together now. Why don't I call you?"

She was silent as he looked down at her. "I'm sorry. I'm sure you understand I've got to make it up to them. I want my kids to have good memories of family and Christmas when they grow up."

"I understand."

Rafe released her to search for the newspaper that listed the times and prices of the Ice Capades, then called to ask about the availability of tickets for Friday. Since he didn't ask Melissa if she wanted to go, she knew she might not hear from him until the weekend.

When he got out a pile of catalogs to look at computer modems, Melissa went to the bedroom to dress, all the while sadly wondering if she'd have any more holiday time with Rafe at all. When would he call her? She'd said she understood his devotion to his children and she'd been telling the truth. But why couldn't he include her in outings with them? And couldn't she and Rafe continue with a few outings of their own, alone? He didn't need every minute with his kids, did he? Wasn't he willing to fit her in somewhere?

"Melissa," Rafe said as he entered the bedroom to find her zipping up her pink tulle fairy dress. "What do you want to do tonight? Shall we go out? Would you like to stop at your place and change clothes first?"

"I'd like more comfortable clothing," she admitted as he put his arms around her. "But there's not much to do on Christmas Day."

"We'll either find an open restaurant or I'll make you a fabulous dinner."

"Sounds good." She nestled her head against his chest,

willing herself to forget her disappointment about the abrupt cancellation of their holiday plans. At least they would have this one night together. And she'd feel guilty if she let herself actually be resentful of two children.

CHAPTER EIGHT

"What's a wicket stepmother?" Gretta asked, startling Melissa as she was tucking the girl into bed. Though Gretta looked at her with wide innocent eyes, the question was loaded.

"A wicked stepmother?"

"Uh huh. Hank said he didn't want no wicket stepmother, but Daddy might get one anyhow. Hank wouldn't tell me what it was." Gretta frowned, making her dark brows draw together. "He told me to read the fairy-tale book you bought me for Christmas, but I don't read so good yet."

Trying to keep her voice light, Melissa said, "When a father gets remarried after his wife dies or after a divorce, his new wife is called a stepmother. She's like a second mother to his children. In fairy tales sometimes the stepmother is mean and nasty and makes the kids miserable. That's why she's called a wicked stepmother. But that's only a story, sweetie. Lots of stepmothers love their husbands' children very much, just like they're their own."

"Well, I don't want a wicked stepmother either." Gretta's dark eyes filled with tears. "You don't think Daddy will get one, do you?"

"If your father ever remarries," Melissa said reassuringly, ruffling the little girl's bangs, "it will be to someone who would love you, Gretta."

"But I already got a mommy who loves me!"

"I know you do, sweetie." Not knowing what else to say, Melissa bent over to kiss Gretta and was warmed by the little girl's big hug. "Sweet dreams."

"Night, Melissa."

Thoughtfully, Melissa left the room, then leaned against the bedroom door after closing it. The last month since the children had come back from California hadn't been easy for her. Just when her relationship with Rafe had been progressing to new intimate and emotional levels and they had needed time together to explore them further they'd had to bring things pretty much to a halt. Now Gretta's innocent questioning made her realize how much more difficult her relationship with Rafe could get.

Or, rather, how much more difficult Hank could make it.

She hadn't been blind to the way Rafe's son used his clever intelligence to manipulate his father, using subtle ploys to keep Rafe's attention on himself and off Melissa on those occasions when they all spent time together. The kid had even had the nerve to invite himself along on two of their dates when the couple had made plans to spend time alone.

Once Hank had pretended he was very interested in the modern art exhibit they were going to see. He'd nagged at his father until he was given permission to come along. Then he'd made Rafe explain the meaning of every painting they saw, leaving him no opportunity to talk to Melissa.

Another time he'd insisted on tagging along with them to a foreign film so he could practice his French. He'd convinced Rafe it was necessary if he were to pass the class. She couldn't believe it when the kid actually sat between them, complaining about the height of the people in front of the other two seats.

If he'd handled those situations adeptly, the computer scheme had been his most clever ploy. When Rafe had to cancel their date the Sunday before, it had been because his computer files with his business records had gotten messed up. He'd blamed himself, saying he must have been really tired or distracted because of the kids' problems. Since his appointment with his tax accountant was scheduled for that week, Rafe had had to stay home to straighten things out.

Later he'd told her Hank volunteered to help him and the job had been completed quickly. In reward he'd taken his son to a hockey game. When he'd bragged about his kid's responsibility and intelligence, Melissa had merely smiled without saying anything. She was sure Hank had been responsible for the foul-up, but she doubted Rafe would believe it. The doting father thought his children could do no wrong. In any case she wouldn't think of telling him something so negative about his son.

There were days when she could swear Hank liked her, but it seemed that every time he was nice to her, he had to do something contrary to make up for it. It hurt Melissa because she was already fond of both children, though Gretta was far easier to love. Knowing Hank's problems stemmed from feeling deprived by his parents' divorce didn't help. How was she supposed to deal with the sticky situation, especially now that he was trying to turn Gretta against her?

Wicked stepmother indeed!

With a sigh she headed down the stairs, wondering what it would take to win Hank over, or if she'd ever succeed. If not, how could her relationship with his father progress?

"What's keeping you?" Rafe demanded, bounding up the stairs and catching Melissa in his arms at the halfway point. His kiss was short but passionate. "I'm ready to go."

"Does that mean what I think it does?"

Melissa rubbed her body invitingly against his while nipping, then kissing, his lower lip. Rafe had promised to take her home for a romantic tryst. It had been difficult to arrange time alone, and they were both eager to further explore their magical lovemaking. Hands on her buttocks, he pressed her lower body into his, allowing her to feel his meaning.

"Do I have to be more specific?"

Melissa tingled with fevered expectancy from the roots of her hair to the tips of her toes. Rafe's state of arousal was achingly obvious even through their clothing, and she was eager to be alone with him. About to say something naughty, she hesitated when she spotted a movement from the corner of her eye. Looking up, she saw Hank leaning over the railing, a sour expression on his face. How long had he been spying on them?

"Hey, Dad, if you're through fooling around, could you help me with my math?"

Rafe immediately let go of Melissa. "Uh, can't it wait until tomorrow?"

"The test is tomorrow. Aw, that's okay if you don't want to help me," the boy said, turning his face into a mask of disappointment. "I guess I won't flunk."

Knowing math was Hank's best subject, Melissa recognized the ploy for what it was. But, as usual, Rafe refused to. He looked at her as if to ask for permission, a plea for understanding in his eyes. She shrugged in acceptance and tried to smile, hoping her expression didn't resemble a grimace.

"All right, Hank. But I have to take Melissa home, first."

"Aw, Dad."

"I'll be back in a half hour," Rafe told him firmly, already heading back down the stairs.

It was Melissa who caught the sly triumph briefly reflected on Hank's face.

"Listen, I'd better not come up," Rafe said when the taxi pulled in front of her building after the short, silent ride. "I'd never get home if I did."

"I wouldn't even try to convince you. I don't have the powers of persuasion Hank does."

Without looking at Rafe, Melissa opened the door, but

124

before she could get out he stayed her with a firm grip on her upper arm. "Try to understand," he begged. "The math test is important to Hank."

"Right." She tried to leave again, but he wouldn't let go.

"I'll make it up to you. I promise. Be patient, Melissa, please. You're just as important to me as the kids are. But we're adults. We can make a few concessions for them, especially now, when they're still so unhappy. It won't last forever."

Melissa said nothing, but allowed Rafe to turn her head so he could kiss her before she left the cab. She ran up the stairs to her refuge where she could think in peace. Would Hank succeed in causing real problems in her relationship with his father? How much longer could she tolerate his childish manipulations and his father's blind devotion? If she said something to Rafe would he believe her? What would Hank do next?

In the following weeks it seemed that Hank would do nothing at all to impede her growing relationship with Rafe. Perhaps he was satisfied with his display of power over his father, Melissa thought, unable to figure out why the boy was extra nice to her in addition. He and Gretta even gave her Valentine cards. She spent more time at the brownstone and Hank adopted the friendlier attitude he'd had before the disastrous holidays, demonstrating computer games he'd programmed using the book she'd given him for Christmas. Was Hank finally accepting her? Melissa wondered, happily contemplating the future. She suspected she was in love and was sure Rafe felt the same. Anything was possible.

Everything was going her way, she decided, straightening her apartment late on a Saturday afternoon. She'd had a job offer for a full-time teaching position the week before. Unfortunately, it was in Pennsylvania. The principal at her old school wanted Melissa to replace a retiring teacher. She'd been elated at the offer, but did she really want to leave just when things seemed to be working out? Uncertain, she'd said nothing to Rafe.

When the phone rang she assumed it was he, calling to make some kind of last-minute plans for the evening. "Hello, you sexy man. What's your pleasure?"

"Uh, if I told you, Rafe would punch me out," came the reply that made Melissa want to die of embarrassment.

"Hux?" she squeaked.

Laughing, he asked, "Hey, remember that promotions idea I had? If you're still interested I think you'd make a classy storytelling fairy to give our toy department the boost it needs on Sunday afternoons and Thursday nights. And there might be more work as well in personal appearances later. Can you come down to the store on Wednesday to negotiate, say three-thirty?"

Was she interested? She wouldn't have to pass out food samples in grocery stores anymore! "Absolutely! See you then. Thanks, Hux."

After hanging up, Melissa dialed Rafe's number.

"Yeah?" came the answering reply.

"Hank? Is your dad there?"

"Naw. He's out."

"Well, can you give him a message? It's real important."

After a slight hesitation, he grunted, "I suppose."

Her elation at her news making her oblivious to his sullen tone, Melissa told him, "Hux offered me a promotions job. I don't know what hours I'll be working, but tomorrow might be my last Sunday off for a while, so I'd like to do something to celebrate. Would you tell your dad to call me as soon as he gets home?"

"Bambi said they're going out to dinner. I don't know what time he'll be home."

"Oh, I see," was all Melissa could say to that announcement.

"Well, I gotta go now."

Stunned, she hung up. Bambi? Rafe was going out with someone named Bambi?

Melissa told herself not to jump to any conclusions, but that was impossible. To get her mind off the idea of Rafe seeing another woman, probably some glamorous model, she decided to take in an early movie. Later, she could barely remember the plot.

After a virtually sleepless night she agreed to go out to breakfast with Terry. Though she merely picked at her food she was happy to listen to him talk so she didn't have to think. Terry told her all about the act he and Clarence were in at one of the more unusual art clubs in Soho. Not exactly Broadway, but it kept them in the business, he told her. She promised she'd come to see them.

Afterward, two hours spent in her apartment waiting for Rafe's call did Melissa's disposition little good. Unwilling to waste the rest of what might be her last free Sunday, she decided to visit the Metropolitan Museum of Art. It was after five when she got home. Exhausted, she finally was able to sleep.

Sometime later she practically jumped off her futon when a noise startled her awake. Groggily, Melissa fumbled around for a light when the buzzer shrilled, alerting her to company.

"Who's there?" she croaked into the intercom.

"It's Rafe."

Tempted to let him stew standing around in her vestibule, Melissa hesitated answering long enough that he signaled her again. She buzzed him up, then trudged through the kitchen to open the door. It was obvious he didn't discern her cranky mood, for he kissed her as though nothing was wrong and didn't seem to notice she wasn't kissing him back.

"Where have you been? I called you last night and several times today."

"Really? You called me last night? In front of your date?"

"My what?" Rafe asked and tried to slip his arms around her waist. "What are you talking about?"

Melissa pulled away abruptly, angry with herself for reacting so strongly to his touch. "You mean who, don't you?" She pronounced the name with unveiled hostility, "Bambi."

Rafe laughed heartily. "How do you know about Bambi?"

"I can't believe you think this is funny, Rafe Damon! I thought I meant something to you, but when I call you to tell you my good news, I find out you're seeing someone else."

Her admonishment made him laugh even harder. "She's a model!" he finally choked out.

Hadn't she known it? Melissa's angry expression dissolved into one of defeat and she felt tears well in her eyes. How was she supposed to compete against some glamorous, sophisticated woman? She was so distraught she didn't even slap Rafe's hand away when he took her by the chin to lift her head.

"Bambi," he said distinctly with a broad smile, "is eleven years old."

"What?"

Taking advantage of her shock, Rafe put his arms around her. "Silly, I told you I mainly work with kids. After shooting a jeans ad we had a business dinner with her mother and her new agent, who also happens to be her new stepfather. Bambi's mom just got remarried—for the third time."

"Oh." Feeling extremely foolish, Melissa frowned up into his amused face.

"Maybe that's why her mother spoils her so badly, to make up for her changing fathers. Whatever Bambi wants, Bambi gets."

"Spoiling a child is as bad as neglecting one," Melissa said, wondering how Rafe could miss the similarities to his own family situation. "It's not the right kind of attention. Presents don't heal emotional wounds."

"Maybe you should talk to Bambi's mother."

Her meaning had gone over his head, she realized in frustration. "I don't care about Bambi. I want to know why Hank didn't tell me you were having a business dinner. He made it sound like you were on a date."

"He probably didn't think to explain. Maybe he assumed you knew who I was working with yesterday afternoon."

Melissa's eyes widened as realization set in. "No, that's not it. He wanted me to assume exactly what I did."

"Don't be silly."

How could Hank have been so cruel as to make her think his father was dating someone else, she wondered, when she'd always been so nice to the boy? So far she'd avoided saying anything about his pranks because she hadn't wanted to cause trouble between father and son. But this time the kid had gone too far and it was clear his behavior was getting worse. To heck with the principles that bade her say only good about others!

"Rafe, you've got to talk with Hank about this. You can't let him off the hook."

"Don't be silly. Hank didn't lie to you." Rafe kissed her on the tip of the nose and smoothed her hair placatingly. "Why are you making a big deal out of a little misunderstanding?"

Melissa ducked her head so his hand slid to her shoulder. Deciding to change tactics, she asked, "Where were you today?"

"I took the kids down to the South Seaport area." Seeming relieved she'd dropped the criticism of his son, Rafe hugged her tightly and rubbed his cheek against her hair. "I called to invite you last night and again this morning, but you weren't in. I really wanted you to go with us."

"But Hank didn't," Melissa muttered, wanting only to melt in her lover's arms instead of fighting with him. But she couldn't give up just yet. How could the man be so blind? She pulled away slightly and backed up in an attempt to lessen Rafe's sensual effect on her so she could discuss the situation rationally. "Your son's been trying to keep us apart. At times, rather successfully."

"Oh, come on. You're imagining things, Melissa. He and Gretta both need extra attention now, but Hank would never—"

"Did he give you my message?"

"What message?"

"I called last night to share some good news with you. Hux has a promotions job for me. That means I don't have to worry about money for a while, but it also means I might not have another Sunday off for a long time. I wanted to celebrate with you today. I told Hank to give you the message, but he didn't, did he?"

Rafe's handsome brow wrinkled, and yet he said, "Hank probably forgot. He's only a kid, you know. From parental experience I can tell you they're not always reliable, no matter how responsible you expect them to be."

Shaking her head, Melissa wished she could figure out how to make Rafe believe her. An impossible task, it seemed. No matter what she said he'd find a way to absolve his son of guilt. She tried to back away from him once more but was stopped by her counter/tub. Rafe followed her movement and pressed himself up against her, sliding his hands up along her waist until he cupped the sides of her breasts.

"Melissa, we weren't able to spend the day together, but we could find ways to make up for that in the next few hours," Rafe coaxed, flicking his thumbs over her nipples. "Why waste our time arguing?"

Why indeed? Melissa wondered, mesmerized by his bedroom eyes, seduced by his hands, which made her breasts throb so achingly. How could he make her insides melt and her toes tingle so easily? Was it because she was in love?

"I don't want to argue," she breathlessly admitted.

"Good. Neither do I. I only want to love you," he murmured, bending his head to kiss her passionately.

He pressed against her, and Melissa gripped him tightly around the neck, as if her embrace could stop Hank from driving them apart. Rafe wouldn't slip away from her, not if she could help it. He might never have that talk with his son . . . but she certainly would.

Realizing her legs were growing weak because the circulation was being cut off by the wooden planks behind her, she murmured in protest, "If we don't get out of here, we're going to be making love on top of my bathtub."

"Hmm." Rafe's dark eyes wickedly lit with mischief. "How many opportunities does a guy get to make love in both the kitchen and bathroom at the same time?"

Thinking about talking honestly with Hank Damon and actually carrying through with the idea were two different things, Melissa learned several days later as she stood outside the boy's bedroom door. She hadn't realized how hard it would be, even knowing that further unpleasantness might develop between them. But right now the timing was perfect. She could get the confrontation over with while Rafe was showering and dressing for their date. Before losing her nerve, she knocked on Hank's door.

"Dad?" His voice sounded eager.

"No, it's Melissa. May I come in?"

"Yeah, I guess so."

Hank watched Melissa suspiciously when she closed the door behind her, leaned on it, and announced, "It's time you and I had a talk, Hank."

"I don't have time," he said, quickly scrambling over to his computer. "I've got homework."

"I'm not about to talk to your back. Look at me."

Hank froze at her determined tone and reluctantly faced her. At first his face reflected a combination of regret and

131

intimidation, but he quickly hid his weaknesses from her. With a great deal of drama, he huffed himself down to the nearest carpeted stair and crossed his arms. "What?"

"Why didn't you tell your father I called Saturday night?"

"I forgot."

"The heck you did!" Melissa stared at him sternly. "Not only did you not forget to tell him, Hank, you deliberately led me to believe he was out on a date."

Hank studied the carpeting and tried to bluff his way around her accusation. "I can't help it if you don't know who Bambi is." She could see his throat muscles tighten as she came closer and stood over him with her arms crossed. "I didn't lie."

"Not directly, perhaps, but the result was the same. What you did was wrong, Hank, and I think you know it."

"I didn't do anything wrong," he insisted sullenly, pulling at a strand of the shag carpeting. "You misunderstood me."

"Did I also misunderstand the purpose for the tape recorder you hid under the couch a few days before Christmas?"

Hank whipped his head up, his eyes wide. He looked panic-stricken and unable to hide it. "I don't know what you're talking about!" he shouted, jerking up from his perch on the step.

"And how about the computer files?" she asked as he began to pace up and down the carpeted levels of his room with increasing agitation. "That was far more clever and infinitely more entertaining than going to see a French movie or an art exhibit."

From his expression it was obvious the boy was appalled she'd found him out. Hank was speechless, but only for a moment. "I suppose you've told my dad," he said, picking up one of his robots. She could sense the tension in his hands as he fondled the prized possession.

132

"No. As a matter of fact, I haven't." Noting the relief spreading through his body, Melissa thought perhaps she could call a truce. "And for the moment, I don't plan to."

"Good. 'Cause there's nothing to tell."

"Yes there is, Hank. You and I both know it. I haven't made an issue of it because I know you've been unhappy and I didn't want to cause hard feelings between your dad and you." Uncrossing her arms, she stepped up to Hank's eye level, but he avoided looking at her, concentrating instead on the robot. "You've been inexcusably rude to me, Hank, and you've played mean tricks on us both. That kind of behavior has got to stop. It won't make anyone happy. Not even you."

"I don't have to listen to you. You're not my mom."

"No, I'm not. But I love your dad, Hank, just as your mother loves her boyfriend, Simon."

"She doesn't! Mom is lonely, that's all. And so's Dad. They're not going to marry other people like that stupid Bambi said. If Mom hadn't moved to California, things'd be different!"

"Maybe they would, but I'm not convinced of it. Hank, I want you to know I care about you and Gretta. Honestly." He stiffened when she touched his arm. "Please don't treat me like a wicked stepmother."

Reddening, Hank abruptly pulled away and aimed a vicious glare at her, then threw the robot down in disgust, unblinking when it broke into several pieces. But it would have been difficult to miss the welling tears in his eyes. "I got homework."

Melissa sighed as he sat down in front of his computer, his stiff back to her. Knowing she wasn't about to get an apology or even a confession out of the boy, she headed for the door, but she made one last plea before going through it. "Think about what I said, Hank. I do care."

She heard him sniffle and mutter something about crummy allergies just before closing the door.

Distracted by her disappointment, Melissa had little to say to Rafe and Louise as they had a drink in front of the fireplace while talking about their day's activities. Would there be many more of these cozy threesomes? she wondered, fondly gazing at her lover and his mother.

Though she no longer felt like going to see Clarence and Terry's club act tonight, she had promised, and she wanted to be supportive of the two people who'd proven to be such good friends. Since Rafe wasn't much of a night nor a club person, she knew he must feel the same or he would have tried to talk her out of going.

When he suggested they get started, Melissa realized it was the first time she'd felt relieved to leave his home. How sad. Forcing a smile, she repeated Terry's directions to get to Tinkerbell's.

"That's in a pretty seedy neighborhood," Rafe said as the taxi pulled away from the curb.

"I know. Most of those crazy new clubs are. This one's housed in a huge old warehouse. Terry told me it's spread over three floors. Live bands play on the first floor. There's an art gallery on the second, and the cabaret where they perform is on the third."

"Sounds like something Hux would like. I wonder if he's been there?"

Several minutes later the cab pulled up to a deserted-looking warehouse.

"Are you sure this is the right place, Melissa? Shouldn't there be lines of people outside? Maybe you'd better check the address," he said dubiously.

"This is the place, but we're early. It's not quite eleven. That's when the place starts jumping, or so Terry told me." Melissa had regained some of her enthusiasm for the evening out. "It should be interesting."

After Rafe paid the exorbitant entry fee she found out how much so. A band was tuning up, its members dressed in garish fifties garb, their hair dyed and chopped. But then, how many customers looked much different? What about the woman in the see-through tinted plastic dress? Or the guy in sequined evening clothes with four inches of glitter-dusted white hair that stood straight up?

Melissa gulped and glanced at Rafe in concern. This was definitely not his kind of scene any more than it was hers. Perhaps if she tried to make the best of it, tried to make it fun for him, they could both have a good time. After all, who knew how many chances she had left. . . .

Rafe gazed around, then blinked in astonishment at what was obviously a male couple in drag. Why hadn't he guessed the place would be so wild? The heavy metal band blasted the first chords of its opening number. Good Lord, he thought, how was he going to stand it? Glancing at Melissa, who was beaming up at him, he had a hard time keeping a frown from his face. Would she really enjoy a place like this?

"Why don't we go up and take a look at the art?"

Melissa nodded enthusiastically. Amazed she'd heard him over the raucous noise, Rafe put a protective arm around her and led the way to the stairs. Once on the second floor, however, he realized the change of scene wasn't much of an improvement. The wooden floor vibrated beneath his feet and the metallic screech of a guitar echoing up from the stairwell made him grit his teeth.

He tried focusing his attention on the enormous display of paintings and sculptures that had no discernable relationship to the world he knew. This was art? Then he noted a couple in a corner. Dressed in black leather and metal chains and spikes, they stood frozen like two mannequins. Were they part of the display? Did the brilliantly colored decorative designs on their faces and bodies come off or were they tattooed on?

"Look, they're alive!" Melissa whispered excitedly, gripping his arm. "Isn't this fun?"

Rafe shuddered and made a noncommittal noise, but

when he looked down into her pretty smiling face with its softly dimpled cheek, his resistance began to melt. Maybe he should try to relax and enjoy himself for her sake. "Definitely unique."

A quarter of an hour later they headed up to the third floor for the cabaret show. The walls were decorated with graffiti art, as were the small cocktail tables and waiters. Even the neon signs over the bar were twisted glass graffiti.

"Oh, look!" Melissa said, wonder—or was it stunned amazement?—widening her eyes. "Have you ever seen anything like this place?"

"Unique," he told her with credible enthusiasm. "Definitely unique."

The show, too, was unique—he'd never seen anything like it. Rafe forced himself to laugh in all the supposedly appropriate places when a guy in drag imitated a rock star. Then they saw a fashion show of sorts when a New Wave designer introduced his skimpy leather loungewear.

When Melissa glanced at him to see his reaction, he nodded and muttered, "Undoubtedly unique," but he was beginning to wonder about his lover's taste in entertainment.

How could anyone over twenty-two enjoy a place like this? he wondered, then remembered he'd thought Melissa was that young when he'd first met her. Though he knew her chronological age, Rafe had difficulty remembering it at times. Her kooky jobs, the way she gave away money when she couldn't afford it, her almost transient apartment, and now this fascination with the bizarre added up to a single question, one that worried him: What was he, the mature, responsible father of two, doing in a relationship with such a free spirit?

Yet just looking at her, with her golden hair, blue eyes, and ready smile, made his heart pound painfully, made him want to carry her out of the place and back to her apartment where he could make love to her. It wasn't merely physical attraction. There was a softness about Melissa that brought out his protective instincts. She was a caring person. A loving person. *Loving.* Yes, there was that, Rafe thought, wondering why it had taken him so long to fully understand the effects her magic had worked on him.

How odd that it would be in this strange place that he would realize he was in love with Melissa Ryan.

Why was he looking at her so strangely? Melissa wondered. Did Rafe hate this place so much? He looked away uneasily, making her cringe. Obviously her ruse to make him think she was having a good time had worked.

"Rafe, I want you to know I don't—" But Melissa's confession of the fact was interrupted by the grand finale.

"Here's the act you've been waiting for folks, Tinkerbell's reggae version of a popular forties movie that takes place in the Caribbean—*The Wizardess of Foz!*"

The music made conversation impossible, so Melissa settled in as a saronged Dorothy cried in a Jamaican accent, "Ahh, look, Toto, here it is—the red coral road."

Stuffed toy dog in arm, Dorothy reggaed down an imaginary path toward the island of Foz, joined by other characters along the way. Clarence played a sun-loving Cowardly Lion complete with dark glasses, beach towel, and rum punch glass, and Terry played a spindly-legged Scarecrow challenging everyone to a limbo contest. Although the act was as offbeat as the others had been, Melissa truly began to enjoy herself, easily laughing at the antics of her friends and humming along to the musical numbers done with a reggae beat, backed by a steel drum band.

"Somewhere, out in the ocean . . . away from the city . . .
There's an island I heard of . . . once in a ditty.
Somewhere, out in the ocean . . . seagulls fly.
Gulls fly over the islands . . . why, oh why, can't I?"

When the act ended Melissa stood with the rest of the crowd, wildly applauding her friends. "Weren't they great?" she asked Rafe with genuine pleasure.

He, too, stood and applauded, though she judged it to be with far less enthusiasm. "I wouldn't have figured Clarence would want to associate himself with this kind of production at his age," Rafe commented.

Was that another criticism, Melissa wondered, or was she being too sensitive? About to suggest they have a drink with her friends, she changed her mind. Even though he didn't voice them on the way home, she was sure of Rafe's negative thoughts about the evening. There was a strangely charged atmosphere around him. Had he come to some unpleasant conclusions concerning her?

Stop it, Melissa scolded herself, realizing she was borrowing trouble. Was she determined to spoil the remainder of the night? Maybe she was being fatalistic, but she viewed the evening as the start of the end of their relationship even though she'd finally been able to admit she loved Rafe. How ironic she'd done so to the son rather than the father.

Sadly remembering her futile talk with Hank, Melissa reminded herself that was why her mood was so negative. And yet, added to the boy's refusal to admit any wrongdoing, there was Rafe's own blindness about his kids. Could she make him open his eyes? Would she be happy making him face something he didn't want to see? She'd never be happy in their relationship unless he did.

Then there was this disaster of a date, probably another of her shortcomings by his "mature" standards. Why couldn't they have taken the bizarre club in the spirit of fun instead of carefully walking through disconnected scenarios grunting pleasantries at each other as if they were strangers thrown together under unfortunate circumstances? Was that his fault or hers? She was being supportive of her friends. Did Rafe disapprove of them as well as her apartment, furniture, and jobs?

Melissa hadn't yet told him about the teaching position in Pennsylvania. Would he congratulate her? Ask her to turn down the offer? If she said she wasn't going to take it, would he see it as proof of her not wanting the responsibility of a full-time job? Melissa didn't have the heart to bring up the subject.

"I think I'm finally getting used to all these stairs," he told her a short while later when they reached her apartment. "I'm hardly huffing and puffing anymore."

Rafe's attempt at humor barely touched her as she fumbled with her keys. He seemed strangely anxious—was he going to say good-bye for good?

"Let me." Taking the keys, he opened the door and turned on the light. "What's wrong, my sugarplum?" Rafe asked, nuzzling the back of her neck as she bolted the door. "You've been so quiet."

"Oh, Rafe, about this evening . . ."

"Shh. Not all our dates can be perfect. What's important is that we spent the time together." He turned her around, and, pressing her against the door, kissed her tenderly. "I want to spend all the time I can with the woman I love."

"What?"

"I love you."

"You do? So do I. Love you, I mean."

"Then let's go tell each other in a hundred different ways," he said, lifting her easily and quickly carrying her to her futon, where he set her down only to throw his body over hers. "I'll bet you didn't know I had a little fairy dust of my own."

"Uh uh. I guess you'll have to demonstrate your magic," Melissa said with a sigh as he proceeded to do so, touching and stroking her until twinkling lights seemed to surround them. Their lovemaking was tender, unlike their usual joyous, playful unions.

139

But afterward, while lying in his arms, she realistically considered her situation. When she'd tried to tell him about Hank's intervention, Rafe had refused to take the accusation seriously. His son had refused to be honest. A less cautious woman might plunge ahead regardless of the consequences, assuming everything would work out for the best. But without Rafe's cooperation, Melissa knew she'd be miserable, fighting a losing battle. Could she really allow that to happen to herself? To him? To the kids?

Snuggling closer to her lover, Melissa felt this night would hold bittersweet memories, made all the more painful because she was so sure this was one time love wouldn't conquer all.

CHAPTER NINE

"I don't like this place," Gretta complained peevishly. "I want to go home!"

"Oh, come on, sweetheart," Rafe said. "You enjoy eating out and I know you like Italian food. Look here"—he pointed at the menu—"they've got linguine cooked with butter and garlic—one of your favorites."

"I don't want it!" the child insisted, kicking her feet against the bottom of the booth's seat as she leaned against her father.

"I don't like anything either," said Hank. "I'm not in the mood—"

"Well, you'd better get in the mood fast," Rafe told him sternly. "I assured Melissa you both liked to eat Italian food. That's why she suggested this restaurant for us."

The two kids quieted then, although Gretta had her lower lip stuck out belligerently as she continued to kick her feet. Hank kept his eyes glued to the menu and didn't look at Melissa, seated beside him.

She sighed. Although she'd given up trying to win the approval of Rafe's family, she'd accepted his invitation and suggested a restaurant for tonight anyway, hoping for the best. But Hank had continued to be covertly hostile—he hadn't looked her in the eye or spoken directly to her since their talk last week—and it seemed he'd finally managed to influence his sister.

On the ride to the restaurant Gretta had refused to give

141

Melissa her usual welcoming hug. Then the child had insisted on riding in the front seat of Rafe's car and inserting herself between the two adults. Clinging tenaciously to her father, Gretta had merely frowned at Melissa.

The kids seemed determined to reject the cozy, family-style Italian restaurant, and Melissa suspected their objections were based on the fact she'd chosen the place. She could only hope they'd settle down once they had some food in their stomachs.

Rafe told Gretta, "You're going to have the linguine—"

But he was interrupted by a man who stuck his head around the booth's corner. "Will you quit the kicking back there? We're trying to have a quiet meal." Rafe nodded and scowled at his daughter.

"I gotta go to the bathroom!" Gretta cried.

"Why didn't you say so before?"

"I didn't know it till now."

Melissa said, "I'll go with her, Rafe. Will you order me some—"

"I don't want to go with *her!*"

Taken aback at the child's strident tone and the way Gretta glared at her, Melissa was speechless and hurt. Gretta had never acted this way around her before. Didn't Rafe notice the change in his daughter's behavior?

"Someone has to accompany you, Gretta, and I can't go into the ladies' room," Rafe said.

"Don't worry, Dad. I was just over there and it's a one-person bathroom," Hank said. "She can go in and I can stand on guard outside the door."

"Well, okay. You take her." Rafe rose to let the child out. "What do you want for dinner, Hank? I'll order for you."

"I'll have the linguine too."

Rafe shook his head at Melissa. After the waitress had taken their orders and left, he apologized for his kids' conduct. "I think they must be tired."

Melissa knew it was more than that. There was no use

142

voicing her suspicions to Rafe, however. She was sure he would find no fault with his children, even if their rejection of his girlfriend led to the end of the love relationship.

"I wish we were sitting side by side," Rafe said, extending his arm across the red tablecloth to cover her hand with his own.

"So do I." She gazed sadly into his dark eyes and thought about how their mutual love would make parting bittersweet. Yet she had to take care of herself, emotionally as well as materially. Although her financial difficulties had been more or less resolved with the new promotions job, she'd also been considering the teaching position that she'd been offered. Perhaps it would be easier to leave the city and her problematic relationship at the same time. Would her lover agree?

"Um, Rafe," she began, wanting to hint at the topic she planned to broach with him later on. "I've received a job offer from my old school in Pennsylvania—a full-time teaching position."

"What?" His brows rose. "You aren't thinking about accepting it, are you?"

"I haven't decided."

"What do you mean you haven't—"

Suddenly they became aware of a noisy commotion coming from the direction of the kitchen. Rafe swiveled in his seat when he recognized Gretta's voice.

"No! Leave me alone!"

Then the kitchen door opened and a man in a white cook's uniform pulled the little girl, kicking and screaming at the top of her lungs, into the dining area. An excited hostess, Rafe, Melissa, and the waitress all gathered to find out what was going on. Other diners openly stared.

"She was in the kitchen," the cook said. "Reaching into a bowl and eating spaghetti with her hands."

Rafe grabbed his child. "Gretta! Come back to the booth

143

and sit down! Why the he—why were you in the kitchen? Where's Hank?"

"I don't know!" Gretta started to cry.

"Damn!" Rafe looked sheepishly at the hostess. "I'm sorry about the trouble. I'll make sure she stays put now."

After leaving Melissa with Gretta beside her in the booth, he went off in search of Hank. Gretta sniffled and pulled away from Melissa's comforting touch. Rafe's raised voice carried across to them as he accompanied his son from the opposite side of the room. Watching the other diners turn to look again, Melissa was embarrassed.

"You are never to leave your sister alone when I ask you to take care of her. Do you understand? You're old enough to know better."

"But I was watching her from the phone, Dad. I just had to make a call to Pete about school."

"I don't care! Did you see Gretta go in the kitchen?"

"Yeah. I didn't think anybody'd hurt her."

"Well, you were supposed to stand by the door and bring her right back. The next time I give you some responsibility, you'd better live up to it!"

"Yeah, Dad. I'm real sorry." Hank looked at the floor.

By the time Rafe and his son were seated again and the curious onlookers had returned to their food, the waitress delivered their salads.

Gretta took one look. "Yuk!" She pushed it toward Hank. Her brother pushed it back, saying, "I don't want it."

As Gretta shoved the bowl at Hank again, Rafe intervened. "I'll eat it. What's the matter with you kids tonight?"

What an awful dinner! Melissa saw that even Rafe was getting thoroughly annoyed. Although she'd been eating in the kitchen, Gretta seemed to be on an intensive hunger strike at the table. Balling up tiny pieces of Italian bread from her side plate, the child threw them at her brother when Rafe wasn't looking and then amused herself by play-

144

ing with the butter. Melissa pretended not to notice. It was up to Rafe to discipline his children, not her. When Gretta's linguine arrived she was relieved to see the child finally take some interest.

"It's delicious," Rafe remarked before he'd hardly taken a bite of his shrimp scampi. Melissa smiled, realizing he was trying to make her feel more at ease.

While Gretta and Hank picked at their food, Melissa ate her sautéed veal and the accompanying pasta. Enjoying the succulent tastes, she began to forget the evening's problems. Perhaps she and Rafe could go out alone for a while after dinner. Any extra hours they could spend together would be a bonus.

"Mom took us for Mexican food in California," Hank stated. "Was it good—especially the cheese enchiladas. You really ought to go with us the next time, Dad."

"I want to go back to Californ'ya!" Gretta chimed in.

"You can go visit your mother again in the summer," Rafe told her.

"Are you gonna come too? Please, please, Daddy," she begged.

"Maybe."

"I wish we could live there," Hank said with a sly expression. "The least you could do is take us yourself and see if you like it."

"We might be able to drive out," Rafe agreed.

Listening silently, Melissa quickly lost her appetite. Placing her fork on her plate, she stared at the veal.

"Oooh!" Gretta said, spitting out food and making a horrible face at her plate.

"What's the matter, honey?" Rafe asked.

"It has mushrooms in it! They're ugly! Yuk!"

Rafe looked. "Great. They're small, but you won't eat them, will you? Either I didn't read the menu well enough or they're not supposed to be there. I'll get the waitress."

"Wait a minute," said Melissa, wanting to avoid attracting attention again. She'd had enough embarrassment for one night. "There are only a few of them," she told Gretta. "We can pick them out."

"I don't want any mushrooms!"

"Scared to try something different?" Melissa asked, trying to challenge the child. "Remember the story I told you about the dragon and his tooth? About how he was scared of changes, of something new?"

"I'm not scared. I just don't like 'em."

"Then eat some and show us how brave you are. We don't know if you can do it."

"Can too!" Scooping up a large forkful, Gretta crammed the food into her mouth. "See?" she taunted, linguine sticking out of the sides of her mouth as she chewed vigorously.

In the meantime Hank was deliberately sorting through the pasta on his own plate, placing bits and pieces of food on the table. "What's the matter with *you* now?" Rafe asked him.

"This has got mushrooms too. I hate mushrooms."

"Come on. You've been eating them already," Rafe said. "They can't be that bad."

"Here, Gretta. You can eat this since you like it so much." With a powerful thrust Hank pushed the plate toward his little sister. But his aim was off. Before Melissa could grab it the heavy plate went over the edge of the table, depositing linguine like a pile of worms into her lap. Feeling like she was living in a nightmare, Melissa watched strands of pasta slither and slide off her corduroy skirt onto the floor.

"Yuk!" she exclaimed, using one of Gretta's favorite words but wishing she could say something stronger.

"Whew! What a night. Thank God it's nice and peaceful here." Sitting in the rocker, Rafe glanced around Melissa's living room as she served coffee with Amaretto on the side. "I'm glad we dropped Hank and Gretta off at the house.

146

They were especially difficult tonight. But that's the way kids get sometimes."

Smiling slightly as she handed him a cup, Melissa said nothing. Did she understand? Living a singles life, she certainly hadn't had the day-to-day hassles of being a parent. Would his kids' less appealing behavior turn her off?

"I know I'm a little overindulgent with them. I've been thinking about that lately and how I ought to talk to them both. Of course problematic behavior is normal for my kids' ages. And Hank and Gretta are dealing with the psychological trauma of divorce, as well."

Melissa seated herself in the sagging director's chair and sipped her coffee, a serious look on her face.

"Aren't you going to say anything?"

"What can I say? It sounds like you have it all figured out."

"Are you being sarcastic?" he asked, wondering what she was getting at.

She sighed. "No, I'm being realistic. I think it's time you were too—about me. Didn't you notice how the kids acted toward me tonight? I don't think they like me and we both should face the fact."

"Is that why you've been so quiet? I told you the kids were tired. They got cranky." She didn't reply, merely gazing at him with solemn blue eyes. Rafe assured her, "You can't take it personally. I'm sure Hank and Gretta like you. They get in their moods, but eventually they'll come around."

"You think so? It sounds like they'd rather move and take you to California to be with Nicole."

"What? Are you worrying about my ex-wife now? I told you I have no interest in her."

"But you *are* planning to take them to visit?"

"I was only humoring them when I said that." Were there unshed tears glittering in Melissa's eyes? he wondered. Was she really so insecure about him? Wanting to comfort her, Rafe rose to lift her from the chair into his arms. "You don't need to be upset. You know I love you. I'm not going anywhere."

"I love you too." Her voice was muffled against his chest. Sniffing a few times, she turned her face toward him and said, "I felt so lonely tonight, so left out."

He stroked her soft hair. "I guess it must be difficult being involved with a man who already has a family and a troubled marital past." She nodded, nestling into him with an unconsciously sensuous movement that made his heart skip a beat. "Everything will work out if we try hard enough, even dealing with the kids. It'll take love, time, and lots of patience. We can't give up so easily—that's what you'd be doing if you took that teaching job in Pennsylvania."

"You don't want me to leave?"

"Of course not, and I don't know why you'd want to go. Haven't we got something special here? I want us to be together, Melissa. I want to be with you so much, I'll take on any obstacle."

Seeing her eyes light up at his words, Rafe lowered his mouth to kiss her. He wished he could ask Melissa to marry him now, but his better judgment told him to wait. It was too soon for a proposal. Years ago he'd made the mistake of rushing a confused Nicole into marriage. This time he wanted to make sure his new love was ready for long-term commitment—and the task of dealing with his kids. Wasn't it enough for them to admit they loved each other at the moment, to agree to try to work things out?

"So you'll forget that job offer?" he asked between kisses. "You'll stay?"

"I never really wanted to take the job. I wanted you to tell me not to leave because our love is so important to you."

"How could you doubt it?" he asked fiercely, tightening his hold as she slipped her arms about his neck. "Every little bit of you is important to me. This part . . . and this one here." She giggled as he pinched her thigh, then cupped her buttocks with his warm hands. Holding her, he felt his heart beat erratically as his passion caught fire. Walking her slowly backward across the room, he lowered her gently onto the futon.

Melissa shivered as Rafe's hand slid beneath her skirt and caressed her from knee to thigh. His fingers roamed possessively over her sensitive flesh, leaving burning trails wherever they touched her.

As she reveled in the delicious sensations, she was also aware of the emotions that had caused them to be amplified so greatly. Rafe had said he wanted her to stay in New York. He wanted them to be together and was willing to deal with any obstacles. With such love and determination, he'd surely be willing to recognize the problem with his children someday. Was he planning to ask her to marry him in the near future? She couldn't help but be excited, although she hoped he'd wait until they'd cleared things up and she felt more comfortable.

Gazing lovingly up at him, she gently stroked his slightly beard-roughened cheek and brushed a lock of dark hair off his forehead. Rafe nibbled at her fingers when they glided over his mouth. Then she moved her hand lower and slid it up beneath his sweater, glorying in his firm muscles, in his smooth skin covered with springy chest hair.

Rafe moaned as her fingers brushed his nipples. "Watch out, little fairy. You're flying too low. This big, bad elf's going to get you."

"You're a prince," she corrected him. "And the fairy's after *you.*" Moving provocatively beneath him, she threw one leg over his hip and felt his arousal pressing hard against her inner thigh.

Quickly—it almost seemed magical—he'd divested them both of their clothing. But the magic didn't stop there. Side by side, warm skin against skin, Rafe kissed her deeply, using his tongue and lips to coax forth exquisite fire. Melissa's breasts seemed to swell beneath his erotic touch, her nipples tightening to hardened buds.

Drifting upward with her spiraling feelings, Melissa saw herself flying over a magical realm full of bright colors. When her lover wooed her flesh with his insistent mouth, seducing her with moist kisses scattered across her midriff and belly, she arched toward him, envisioning the curving rainbow on which her magical kingdom rested.

Rafe continued his loving homage, dipping his head ever nearer her feminine core. As his tongue and lips boldly caressed her there, Melissa's vision began to whirl around them. Like a kaleidoscopic design, dazzling hues whirled and tossed. All of a sudden the rainbow shattered, its colors flaring in a brilliant flash of light.

When her breathing finally slowed, Melissa reached out for Rafe.

He had only begun. "I love you," he whispered, moving over her. Enclosing her tenderly, he joined their bodies to thrust toward the inevitable union that was both earthly magic and yet vastly more than physical.

She watched the rainbow reform itself as he moved within her. Clasping him tightly, she wondered if they would scale the multicolored heights together.

But their erotic journey moved slowly, as if neither wanted it to end. Melissa clung to him, slipping her hands over and over along his damp skin, caressing him as she accepted his searching kisses. Time seemed to stop. Melissa was surprised when everything finally changed and the colors began to wheel and spin once more. Then they both cried out together.

Afterward they lay sated in each other's arms. Holding her closely to him, Rafe growled, "I want a commitment from you."

"Yes?" With a combination of thrill and dread, Melissa

waited for the proposal she was sure would come. What would she say?

"From now on I want you to promise me you'll discuss your doubts with me. You don't have to use some out-of-state job offer to get me to tell you how I feel."

Melissa hadn't really intended to use the job in that way, but she was silent about it, happy that Rafe wanted to improve their communication.

"And when we have problems between us or with anyone else, we'll discuss them openly and decide mutually on solutions."

"That's fine with me." Perhaps now was the time to bring up the kids again, she thought.

But he continued, stating, "Then we both agree to making the commitment. In the meantime I promise to keep you warm. It's getting cold in here." Raising himself on his elbows, Rafe rearranged the bedclothes, tucking them around her.

Smiling at him outwardly, Melissa repressed a sigh that was a mixture of disappointment and relief. He hadn't proposed after all. But she believed he would, just as he'd face the problems with his kids eventually. She was certain marriage was what Rafe intended for them. What else would a man want who admitted he liked to nest, loved kids, and had told Melissa he loved her and wanted them to be together? Would they have their own baby together someday? Simply thinking about it made Melissa feel happy. Unconsciously, she arched her hips against him.

"Again?" he asked. "I'm game."

But the phone rang. "Damn!" cursed Rafe, looking around. "Why are we always being interrupted? Where's your phone, anyway?"

"I'll get it," Melissa told him, scrambling up and stepping over his body. Bare feet chilled by the cold floor, she ran to the living room to pick up the receiver. "Hello?"

"I want to . . . to speak to my dad," sobbed Hank.

"What's wrong?" Melissa thought she could also hear Gretta crying in the background.

"Let me talk to Dad! It's your fault, Melissa!"

When she motioned to him Rafe took only a few seconds to get to the phone. Feeling shaken by Hank's tone and his accusation, Melissa listened, hearing something about mushrooms and food poisoning. As Rafe talked she threw on a pair of jeans and a blouse and got his clothes together.

"I'll be there as soon as I can," Rafe promised, then hung up the receiver. Grabbing his pants and sweater from Melissa, he dressed quickly. "Come on. Hanks says they have botulism from eating the mushrooms. I'll have to take them to the hospital."

"Botulism? That's caused only by canned foods. I'm sure those mushrooms were fresh," she said, but Rafe was already racing out the front door. Hurrying out into the night, they jumped into his car to speed toward the Damon house.

"If it isn't botulism it could be some other kind of food poisoning. Where the hell was Louise?" Rafe muttered, sweat beading on his brow. "Hank said she stepped out. She should have checked on them before she left."

"How do you know she didn't? And maybe she had a quick errand."

"This late?" He checked his watch. "It's almost midnight."

As he swerved to miss a pedestrian Melissa held her breath. "Try not to worry. I'm sure we'll get there on time." She attempted to soothe him.

"I can't help but be worried."

Leaving the car in a no-parking zone, they ran into the town house and climbed the stairs to the second floor. Once there, they found the place in an uproar.

As soon as she saw them Louise approached, holding a bottle of antacid tablets in her hand. "Do you know what these kids have done, Rafe? I was in the entryway downstairs when Hank finished calling you. I overheard the end of the phone conversation. They aren't sick!"

"What do you mean, they're not sick?" Rafe asked.

"They were talking when I came upstairs. They wanted to pretend they had food poisoning so you'd come home. This is too much!"

Gretta appeared then, clutching a doll tightly against her pajama top and crying. "She took us to that place and made us eat mushrooms!" she said accusingly, pointing at Melissa.

"And it didn't hurt you one bit, did it? Do you want to admit that?" Louise asked, showing Gretta the bottle she held. "Or shall I make you take more of this medicine?"

At the threat Gretta wailed louder and Rafe went to pick her up. "There, there," he crooned. "Settle down. Everything's okay."

"Everything is not okay!" exclaimed Louise. "They should be punished."

Melissa agreed. Looking at Rafe, however, she noticed his concern as he quieted the child. Wasn't he angry? Hank and Gretta had accused her of causing them to get food poisoning!

"I'll take care of the kids," he told Louise. "You can get back to bed. Is Hank upstairs?" When his mother nodded yes, he headed up to the third floor, carrying his daughter against his shoulder.

"Really!" Louise looked at Melissa. "Those two children have been terrible. I know they've frightened you with their lies. I'm sorry I wasn't upstairs to stop them from calling you."

"You aren't to blame," Melissa said comfortingly, reaching out to touch Louise's arm. "You can't be around every second."

"I thought Hank was intelligent and old enough to be more responsible."

"He's definitely intelligent," Melissa agreed, thinking

153

about all the brilliant schemes the boy had successfully implemented to keep his father and her apart. If Louise only knew!

"Hank needs guidance," said Louise before going back downstairs.

When Rafe returned from his kids' rooms Melissa was sitting at the kitchen table. He went directly to the refrigerator and took out a pitcher of juice. "Want some?" he asked her, pouring a glass.

"No thanks. How are the kids?"

"Fine. No fever, no spasms. Louise was right, they weren't sick." He smiled tiredly.

Melissa tried to smile too. "So what are you going to do? Did you reprimand them? They gave us a terrible scare."

"I was so relieved they were all right, I didn't have the heart to punish them. I'll have to talk to them later."

Feeling thoroughly aggrieved, she said, "But they've been terrible, Rafe. Do you realize they accused me of causing them to get sick?"

"I know. If they hadn't been so lonely, left in the house by themselves—"

"That's no excuse!" Melissa interrupted him sharply. "And they weren't alone. Louise was downstairs all the time."

"Well, what do you want me to do, spank them?" he asked defensively.

Incredulous, Melissa could say nothing for a moment. Once again Hank had ruined an evening they planned to spend together and had been positively vindictive about it. Didn't Rafe care about her feelings?

Finally she found her voice. "I don't care whether or not you physically punish them, but you certainly ought to tell them how badly they've behaved. They owe me an apology, Rafe."

"I don't think they meant it personally, Melissa. They

154

wanted their dad home, that's all. They don't have their mother anymore."

Melissa almost screamed. Was Rafe really so dense? "They did mean it personally! They wanted their dad to be home so he couldn't be with *me*. How long are you going to use the divorce to excuse them?" She stood up to face him, drawing herself up to her full, if diminutive, height. "Hank's used everything in his power to keep us apart. He's spied and schemed. First, it was a tape recorder. The night before going to California, Hank put one under the couch so he could hear what we were talking about. I found it and turned it off."

"A tape recorder?"

Not stopping to clarify the matter, Melissa went on, "There's a lot more, Rafe. Your son is no angel. He's managed to impose himself on several of our dates. Remember the art show he attended with us and the French movie? He even sabotaged your computer records so we couldn't go out at all. Then he volunteered to aid you in putting them back together. And you rewarded him for it!"

"You're being ridiculous. Hank wouldn't do that," Rafe said, scowling.

"How blind can you be?" She glared at him. "He didn't give you my phone message and deliberately let me think you were out with another woman. How can you let him manipulate you this way?"

"You're exaggerating." His tone was adamant. "I've got two really great kids who also happen to be normal."

"I'm not exaggerating, Rafe. And I don't mean to say Hank isn't a good kid underneath. But he desperately needs to be found out. You may think you're helping your children by being indulgent, but they need discipline and guidance."

Rafe's angry dark eyes seemed to throw off sparks. "Now, wait a minute. You're making serious accusations here. I'm the parent and I know my own kids. Don't tell me how to

155

raise them! Being a teacher for a few years doesn't make you an expert. My kids just need time to adjust."

"How much time?" Undeterred by his anger, she addressed him intently. "You and Nicole divorced more than a year ago. We've been having these problems for almost three months. Tonight you asked me to stay in New York, to commit myself. You said we should discuss problems. Well, Hank and Gretta are a problem if we're ever to get—have a long-term relationship," she stated, not daring to mention the word "marriage."

"I told you there were problems in going out with a divorced man who has a family."

"I expect there to be problems, but I also expect you to try to deal with them!"

"I deal with them as best I can. Children don't disappear, you know. They aren't portable or fleeting like the other things in your transient life-style."

Feeling her face flame with indignation, Melissa tried to control her trembling voice. "I'm neither transient nor irresponsible. I'm not suggesting you put Hank and Gretta in an orphanage. I simply think you should discipline them so they'll grow up to be mature and responsible adults—and we can be happier."

"Happier? How can we be, the way you feel about my kids? Life isn't like one of your fairy tales, Melissa. We're the adults, not Hank and Gretta, and we have to work toward making our happy endings come about. We need to have maturity and insight to deal with children on a day-to-day basis. I don't know if you're ready for that. Isn't it a little immature to be jealous of two kids?"

She couldn't stand it one minute longer. Her anger spilled out in a torrent. "You blind, arrogant fool!" she shouted. "Who are you to accuse me of immaturity or irresponsibility? You refuse to see what's going on right under your nose. Your children are spoiled rotten! What kind of parent does that make you?"

She raced for the door, but before she could descend the stairs he grabbed her by the arm. "Wait a minute," he insisted, his eyes flashing. "We're not through with this! You can't leave in the middle—"

"Are you ready to admit you might be wrong about your precious kids?"

"No!"

Melissa jerked away from him. "Then I'm taking my irresponsible self right out of your life, Rafe. Good-bye!" Running blindly down the stairs, she almost ran into a startled Louise at the bottom of the flight.

Ignoring her humiliation, Melissa rushed past Louise out into the cold New York night, heading toward a busier street to hail a taxi. She brushed at the tears running down her cheeks. Already feeling guilty for her uncharacteristic outburst of rage, she couldn't help but remember Rafe's telling her to be open and to discuss her feelings and doubts. That obviously didn't include his kids!

CHAPTER TEN

"I still haven't found a place to live that I both like and can afford, even though the pay for this promotions job is really good," Melissa complained while walking into Haldan-Northrop after a celebratory lunch. "I can't stand the thought of sharing my living space with rodents."

"Don't give up hope, my girl. Sometimes there's a rainbow at the end of the chase," Clarence replied.

Not wanting to think about rainbows lest they remind her of that last evening with Rafe, Melissa ignored Clarence's heartening comment and led the way past the makeup counter onto the escalator. The sights and sounds of the elegant store were comfortingly familiar, yet she was definitely unsettled as the feeling of loss she'd been trying to repress engulfed her.

"I don't know what I'm going to do if I don't find something I like soon," Melissa said in a desperate attempt to get her mind off of the man she loved. "I've got only three weeks left."

"You can always stay at my place until you can find one of your own," Terry offered.

"I can stay with other friends," Clarence added. "It's no problem, I assure you."

Knowing Clarence was down on his luck again and had been sleeping on Terry's sofa for the last month, Melissa couldn't accept, but neither could she hurt their feelings by refusing outright. "Thanks. I'll think about it, but maybe should go home to Pennsylvania and take that teaching job this fall. I have another few weeks to make the decision," she said bravely, trying to keep her voice from breaking when she added, "Maybe I'm fated to leave New York . . . and Rafe."

"Santa goofed again, the old reprobate. I always hate it when Christmas presents break," Clarence grumbled. "Are you sure the damage is irreparable?"

"Even if Rafe realizes he's wrong about me and the way he spoils his kids things wouldn't work out. Hank and Gretta hate me." Even so, Melissa felt an anticipatory quiver in her stomach as she almost tripped off the moving stairs because she was busy thinking about seeing Rafe shortly. "I'd never be happy causing a rift between the kids and their father. It's bad enough I'm miserable. I don't want to make them all miserable as well."

"Personally, my girl, I think you'll be sorry if you don't persist. I doubt your relationship with the children would remain grim forever. Believe me, it's no fun living your entire life alone because you made one foolish mistake and gave up too easily." Before Melissa could ask Clarence if he was speaking from personal experience, his glance strayed over her shoulder and his eyes lit with a naughty twinkle. "Ahh, my favorite secretary." Off he went.

Terry took Melissa's hands in his own and squeezed them reassuringly. "Remember, you have friends if you need a sympathetic ear, Melissa. And the offer for the place to stay is from the heart. You're welcome anytime."

"Oh, Terry!" Melissa wrapped her arms around her slender friend and hugged him tightly. "You're a dear. Thanks."

After kissing him on his freckled cheek, she headed for the dressing room. Secretly pleased that Rafe had been commissioned to do the publicity layout that would advertise her storytelling hours in newspaper ads and posters to

159

be distributed around the store, Melissa prepared herself with special care.

Her sparkling white costume was almost luminous, studded as it was with tiny crystals and silver bugle beads. Gauzelike beaded wings flowed from the shoulders. Donning it, she thought about how much playing a storytelling fairy for Haldan-Northrop pleased her. Though commercial—she drew kids into the toy department while moms shopped in the rest of the store—her work here was as satisfying as her library job. She was inspiring kids to read by making it fun. That was the important thing. Being a storytelling fairy was a far cry from the odd jobs she'd taken during the past months.

After twisting sprays of crystal drops into her golden tresses, Melissa picked up her silver wand and glanced into the mirror one last time to make sure her appearance was appropriately magical. Not bad. Unable to avoid the inevitable confrontation with the man she loved, she wondered what Rafe would think.

Would he be so happy to see her he'd want to take her in his arms and kiss her?

Would she let him?

Did he still love her?

Taking a deep breath, she decided to find out for herself. It went against her upbringing—not to mention her positive nature—to hold hard feelings against anyone. Though there were certain problems over which she had no control, and though she might want more from him, the least she could do was offer Rafe her friendship, even if it killed her. With that thought Melissa headed for the toy department.

Rafe banged a tripod in place so hard a few of the adults delivering their kids stared at him curiously before turning away. Feeling a flush creep across his face, he wondered what the hell was the matter with him. Why was he so grumpy just because he saw Melissa kissing Terry? He had no claims on her. The fact had been made very clear to him when she'd chosen to walk out of his life two weeks before and hadn't called to apologize since.

Yet, in his mind's eye, he saw her honest blue eyes, her cupid's bow mouth turned up into a sweet smile that dimpled her cheek, her petite body that fit so perfectly with his own.

Truthful with himself, Rafe knew he'd been looking forward to seeing Melissa, had had some vague hope she'd be glad to see him, that she'd want to be with him once more. How foolish could he be? She wasn't exactly pining for male company. He should have known Terry would move in at the first opportunity.

With that in mind, Rafe was in a peculiarly mulish mood by the time Melissa entered the toy department, vaguely staring at her crystal throne as though she was determined to ignore him. Even so, one glance at her absolute loveliness and he dropped his Hasselblad before he could fix it to the tripod.

"Hey, watch it!"

A large hand caught the tumbling camera and held it out to Rafe, who immediately snatched it back. "Don't worry, Hux, I wouldn't bill the store for my own clumsiness."

"Good, because we wouldn't pay for it. Say, I heard you and Melissa broke up a few weeks ago. That right?"

Disliking the sparkle of interest in his friend's green eyes, Rafe growled, "Louise talks too much."

"You really let a honey get away, but I guess I understand it. Getting too serious, right? What man wants to tie himself down to just one sweet, loving woman when he can go out on the town with a different party girl every night of the week? And isn't it great you don't have to feel guilty? I mean, you don't have to worry about her being lonely, because there are plenty of men who'd like to keep that little fairy happy."

161

Rafe scowled in response to Hux's smirk of satisfaction as the other man strolled off toward the fairy in question. Was that a cynic's way of telling him he was a fool?

He glanced at Melissa, now only several yards from his reach. Small kids crowded around her and Hux. She was so enchantingly beautiful in her costume that he could almost believe she really was a fairy. Hadn't she enchanted him over and over again? His heart ached fiercely without her in his life. What did she think about working with him under the circumstances?

What would it be like to take her in his arms again?

Would she melt into him if he did?

Did she still love him?

Taking a deep breath, he decided he wasn't going to get a chance to find out, not here, at least. But perhaps he could persuade her to see him away from the store where they could try to mend their relationship.

Although she greeted the children crowding around her, Melissa was well aware of Rafe Damon's magnetic presence, making it difficult for her to get into her character of Melisande, the fairy she'd chosen to play since her name was so similar. Fool that she was, she'd never thought it would be this difficult to be near Rafe and not be able to smile at him naturally.

"We're going to have a photographer taking pictures today," she told the children, "but we'll try to ignore him, won't we?"

"I'm gonna be a photographer when I grow up!" shouted a boy.

"Me too!" a girl added. "I wanna watch him!"

"He wants to take our pictures as if it was any other storytelling hour. If you all watch him who'll be able to help me talk about the story?"

"I will, Melisande!"

"I will!" exclaimed another child who shoved the first.

162

"Hey, kids, why don't you all sit down quietly?" Hux asked. "I'm going to steal your fairy for a minute."

Angry little faces turned to him and the kids' disapproval was immediately apparent. "You can't steal her. We won't let you!"

"No fair!"

"We'll protect you, Melisande."

"That won't be necessary," Melissa assured them, trying not to grin when she noted Hux's horrified expression. "I promise I'll be right back so we can begin our story. Why don't you try to guess what it will be about?" The challenge worked, appeasing the kids easily. Smiling at their excited murmurs, she followed Hux away from small ears.

"I've got to give you credit for being able to keep control over all those little devils. They're enough to strike fear into a heart braver than mine!"

"If I didn't know you better, I might believe you hated kids."

A reluctant smile lit Hux's face. "How do you know I don't?"

"Hux is a big softie, but don't tell anyone or you'll get me into trouble for ruining his reputation."

Rafe. Melissa's mouth went dry and she suddenly found it difficult to breathe normally as she finally faced him. "Hello, Rafe," she murmured as his dark eyes appraised her.

"Good to see you, Melissa," he replied before hooding his eyes, sheltering his thoughts.

"Now that the introductions are made, can we talk business?" Hux asked dryly. "I've got a gorgeous creature waiting for me downstairs and I don't believe in letting a *good thing* get away."

Why did he look from Rafe to her as though they should get some significance from that statement? Melissa wondered.

"I just wanted to tell you that this session is really impor-

163

tant. I've talked to a friend at *People* and she said we might get a feature if she likes the pictures." Hux glanced at his watch. "Got to get going. You two can continue without my help. I have confidence you'll figure things out eventually."

Melissa frowned as Hux strolled away, a satisfied expression on his handsome face. Unless she was crazy he'd just set them up for a personal confrontation in the middle of a work session. She glanced at Rafe uncertainly.

"Umm, is there anything we need to discuss?"

"You tell me."

Melissa was sure he wasn't thinking of business, but his guarded expression was disconcerting. Perhaps now was a good time to bring up the subject of remaining friends. They could do so in spite of their differences, couldn't they? She couldn't bear the thought of having to see him professionally from time to time, both of them acting like mere acquaintances.

"Well, after all the time we spent together over the past few months, I thought . . . it would be a shame to . . . umm, maybe we still could be friends."

"Friends?" His vehemence startled Melissa, making her think he didn't even want that close an association if she couldn't live up to his standards. Glaring, he added, "You mean like you and Terry?"

She glared back at him. "Terry and I are very close."

"Yeah, I noticed. Have you been seeing a lot of that twerp lately?"

"Twerp? Hey, wait a minute!"

But before she could work up steam, a small voice called, "Melisande?" A freckle-faced girl stood only a few feet away. "Can we have our story now?"

How could she have forgotten where she was? Melissa wondered, following the girl back to the others. After allowing a few of the children guesses as to what kind of a story she would tell, all of which were wrong, she began. Frustrated by the aborted argument she'd been about to enter in defense of her loyal friend, Melissa took pleasure in creating a story especially to irritate the rotten photographer who was presently absorbed in his equipment!

"Once upon a time, there was a bad-tempered ogre who didn't have any friends because he chased people away if they weren't exactly what he thought they should be." Carefully watching for Rafe's reaction, she went on. "Well, this terrible ogre gave little children everything they wanted. He stuffed them with candy and gave them all sorts of toys, but it wasn't for their own good. Someday, he planned to stuff them in a pie and bake them!"

If his stormy expression were any indication, Rafe had gotten the message, Melissa thought, grinning with satisfaction as she continued.

Back in the dressing room, Melissa had some cause to regret letting Rafe Damon goad her as he had. But drat the man, why couldn't he have acted civilized? Didn't he want to be friends? And what about his attitude toward Terry? He'd seemed jealous, for goodness' sake! Sinking down to the bench in front of her locker, Melissa wondered if that weren't significant—did it mean he still cared? Oh, she hoped so, for even as she'd offered her friendship, she'd longed for so much more. How would she go through life without Rafe Damon's love?

Remembering Clarence had told her it wasn't fun to be alone because of a foolish mistake, she thought of calling Rafe and suggesting they try to work out their problems. Having had weeks to think about it, she suspected his views about maturity and responsibility grew out of his negative experiences with Nicole. She'd convince him she wasn't at all like his flighty ex-wife.

And yet Melissa was uneasy about making the first move. After all, he let her walk out of his life without calling to apologize or trying to resolve things between them. Should she wait a while longer to see if he came around? She did have to find an apartment quickly. Perhaps she'd better concentrate on that first. With both her work situation and living arrangements taken care of, Rafe wouldn't be able to criticize her life-style so easily.

Then they could deal with the kids—if Rafe were willing. If he agreed they could talk to the children together. Gretta wasn't heartless, and Melissa didn't think Hank was, either. The positive thoughts lifted her spirits higher than they'd been in weeks.

"Aw, Dad, do we have to go to the museum *and* basketball game with you? Why can't you take someone your own age?" Hank complained with a sour expression. "How about Uncle Hux? Gretta's invited to a birthday party. And Pete's got this neat new war game he wants me to try out with him."

"I thought you liked doing things with me."

"I do. But we haven't seen our friends for a long time."

"You see them every day at school."

"Dad! That's not the same thing."

Trying not to be too relieved that he didn't have to spend another entire Saturday escorting his kids around the city, Rafe said, "All right, fine. I won't make any plans for this weekend then."

He scowled as his son's face lit sunnily and Hank ran back up to the third floor yelling, "Hey, Gretta, we don't have to go to the museum on Saturday!" The kids didn't have to be that thrilled they wouldn't have to spend their free time with him!

Shaking his head, Rafe picked up his newspaper from its resting place on the plush sofa, but the words blurred together before his tired eyes, making reading impossible. How could his life have gone so sour in a few short weeks? He couldn't be less happy. Not only did he not have the woman he loved in his arms because the kids came between them—due to her immaturity, he reminded himself

—but Hank and Gretta were sick of his outings. Now that they'd secured his complete attention, they'd rather be with their friends than with their dad.

He was still staring at the newspaper when Louise came up the stairs humming a cheerful tune. "I'm going to pack lunches for the children, dear. Want a snack?"

"I'm not hungry," Rafe returned grumpily.

Louise approached him, looking at the paper in his hands curiously. "Instead of trying to read an upside-down newspaper, why don't you call Melissa and apologize?" She ignored Rafe's glare as he realized his mistake and quickly refolded the paper.

"I have no reason to apologize."

Crossing her arms, she planted herself firmly in front of him. "I know I promised I'd mind my own business on Christmas Eve, but I can't stand by and watch you wallow in your misery. Call me interfering if you want, but I *am* your mother!"

"I love Melissa, Louise, but you know as well as I do that it will never work out between us. I can't help it if I'm mature and responsible and she's not."

"You and your phobia for responsibility! That girl has more than one job to survive, not because she's irresponsible! Unless I'm crazy you fell for Melissa because of her personality, her charm, and her loving nature, and now you want her to change."

"Our life-styles are too different to—"

"They're not that different. You have more than enough money, she doesn't. That's the biggest difference. If only you hadn't married so young you wouldn't be an old dunderhead before your time." Again Rafe glared and opened his mouth to protest. "Don't give me that look!" she commanded before he could utter a word. "It's the truth! You assumed too much responsibility too soon. You even started a family before you were dry behind the ears—merely because you couldn't control your raging hormones."

"Louise!" Rafe said indignantly, trying to rise.

"Don't Louise me, Raphael Damon!" She pushed him back down. "You hear me out. God knows I love those kids as much as you do. But Melissa, with her unbiased vision as an outsider, recognized the truth—we've spoiled them badly, not only with presents. Now you've allowed them to blackmail you emotionally to the point of cutting the woman you love out of your life. Where does that leave you? They'll have their own lives and loves in a few years. Whom will you have?"

"All right! I love Melissa, and sometimes I think I'll go crazy without her. But love is a damn fairy tale, not reality. I know what's best for my kids," Rafe told his mother belligerently.

"No, I don't think you do. They need discipline as well as love, Rafe. They need to learn the world doesn't revolve around their every whim, because it doesn't. It's up to you to teach them they can't have everything they want—like you and their mother together. Nicole plans to marry Simon this summer, but it doesn't have to be a bad thing for them. Having more than two parents can be a positive experience if you help them see it that way. It's time Hank and Gretta accepted the fact that you need someone to love in addition to them. You need Melissa."

"Are you through?" Too angry at himself to admit his mother was right—hadn't he been coming to the same conclusions, using Melissa's supposed immaturity as an excuse to avoid dealing with the results of overindulging his kids?—Rafe stalked by his mother. "I'm going for a walk."

He heard Louise sigh and softly ask, "When are you going to stop running from the truth? You made one mistake in love. Please don't make another."

Louise wandered toward the stairs leading to the third floor, but passed them and peered out the window. Hearing a sniffle, she turned to see Hank stealthily backing away from the top of the staircase as though he didn't want her to catch him. Had he been listening? She decided to find out for herself. Making her way up the staircase, she didn't pause until she reached his door, where she could hear Hank pacing up and down the carpeted levels of his room. She knocked loudly.

"I'm busy!" he shouted, but she opened the door anyway and walked in.

"Hank, I want to talk to—" Louise paused when she noted him furtively wiping a fist across his eyes. "Honey, what's wrong?"

Hank mumbled, "I caught my finger in one of my robots. It hurt, but it's better now."

"Is it bleeding? Let me see."

"No!" Hank hid a hand behind his back. "It's okay!"

Louise studied him, her dark eyes piercing his, trying to read his troubled thoughts. "Is there something you'd like to talk about, Hank?"

He bit his lip, and she could tell he was trying to prevent tears from giving him away. Boys weren't supposed to cry, were they? she remembered with sympathy. But he was only a child, and the responsibility he'd been shouldering suddenly seemed to overburden him. A dam burst inside her grandson, the evidence flooding through his eyes.

Louise took a step toward him, her arms out. It was all the invitation the boy needed. Hank threw himself tightly into his grandmother's embrace and sobbed uncontrollably.

"Shh, it's okay, honey," she said assuringly, stroking his hair. "Whatever it is will be all right."

"It won't!" he protested, his words muffled by her comforting breast. "Nothing's ever gonna be okay again and it's my fault."

"What is?"

"I tried to be responsible, but I couldn't get them back together. I tried real hard, even when Mom said I couldn't. I didn't believe her 'cause everyone always says I'm real smart and I can do anything I want. But nothing worked like it was supposed to."

His grandmother sat on one of the steps and pulled him down next to her. "That explanation was pretty jumbled, but I think I understand," she said softly, pushing his hair off his forehead.

"I tried to get Mom to come back to New York, but she doesn't want us anymore. She said she and Dad weren't right for each other. They got married too young so they didn't even know it for lots of years. She said she loved me and Gretta, but I don't think so," he said, trying to control a sob. "Why else would she leave us?"

"She does love you, Hank, you've got to believe that. Your mother just never had a chance to grow up before she married. But she finally gave herself that chance when she decided to see if she could make it on her own. I think she'll be happier now. She let your father have custody of you and Gretta because she wanted the best for you, not because she didn't love you."

Hank sobbed harder. "But Dad's gonna hate me when he figures out Melissa's gone 'cause of me. I did really bad things, Gran."

"I know you did, Hank."

"Do you hate me?"

"Of course not. I love you and so does your father."

"He won't. He loves Melissa and he's miserable without her. He doesn't even laugh or anything anymore. Gretta cried last night 'cause I read her a bedtime story and she said she wanted Melissa to do it. And I was glad when she was gone, but I—I don't h-hate her. She knows lots about computers and robots," Hank choked out. Louise knew it was as close as he'd come to saying he, too, missed Melissa. She gave him an encouraging squeeze and he told her, "I heard what you said—I know it's my fault. I'm sorry, Gran."

170

"I'm glad to hear it, Hank. Now, what are you going to do about it?"

Hank hung his head and Louise could tell he dreaded another scene like this one. Sniffling, he told her, "I can't tell Dad. Can you do it for me? Please, Gran?"

Louise lifted his chin and looked into the dark eyes so like those of her son. "Honey, sometimes I think your father's wrong when he expects you to be so responsible, but this time we both know it's up to you to do the right thing."

Gulping hard, Hank nodded. "I just gotta figure out how to fix things."

Because he really was extremely smart like everyone said, Louise was sure it wouldn't take long for Hank to figure out exactly what he had to do.

CHAPTER ELEVEN

"And so the knight made a bargain with the dragon and the monster agreed not to bother the kingdom anymore. Needless to say, everyone was very happy. See the smiles on their faces?" Melissa wound up her library storytelling session by showing the attentive group of children the final colorful pictures in the large illustrated book.

"That's it—the whole story?" asked Michael, a rather sophisticated boy of eight or nine. "It wasn't very interesting."

"I liked it," said a small red-haired girl.

"Maybe you'll be more interested by my story next week, Michael," Melissa suggested. "I plan to tell a different kind each time. Does anyone have questions about 'The Dragon and the Knight,' or something they'd like to say?" As she led the ensuing discussion, her eyes were suddenly drawn by a movement near some shelves nearby. Had she seen a face peek out and then disappear? Was there a shy child lurking over there?

"What happened to the princess?" the red-haired girl asked, pointing to another picture in the book Melissa held.

Melissa started to answer when, to her amazement, she saw Hank shuffle out from behind the shelving units, leading Gretta by the hand. Eyes downcast, the boy looked very uncomfortable. Not knowing exactly what to do, Melissa repressed her thrill of emotion and merely waved hello to them. What were Rafe's kids doing here?

"So what happened to the princess?" the little girl asked again.

"Hmm?" Trying to focus on what the child was saying, Melissa saw Hank and Gretta stop to watch and listen a short distance away. Glancing at the book in her hands, she was struck with sudden inspiration, deciding to embellish the knight and dragon story with a few personalized details of her own.

"What happened to her, Miss Ryan?"

"Well, Brenda," she explained carefully, "the princess waited for the knight, who was also a prince, to get through making his bargain with the dragon. The prince was her own true love, and because of that naughty green monster, the prince and princess had been separated and broken-hearted for a long time."

"Aw, that's sad," remarked Brenda.

"Yuk!" said Michael.

"But eventually the prince and princess got back together. And their love was so beautiful it lit up the kingdom, illuminating everything and everyone. Even the dragon was happier. There's something we can learn from this story—everyone benefits from real love."

Melissa looked directly at Gretta and Hank. The little girl smiled brightly at her, but Rafe's son only looked sheepish and kept a tight hold on his sister's hand. Did they realize she'd added details to the story just for them?

"Oh, boy!" exclaimed Brenda. "Did the prince and princess get married?"

"I'm sure they did."

Michael took the book from Melissa to look at it. "There aren't any pictures in here to show stuff like that happening."

"No, there aren't. And you won't find my entire story in the text of this book either. The chapter about the prince and princess is . . . in another volume."

"Well, it's too mushy for me!" declared Michael, rising

173

from the table to walk away. "There's probably way too much huggin' and kissin'! I'm gonna go look at the superhero comic books."

After Melissa had dismissed the group, passing out a number of books, Hank and Gretta approached her.

"Hello, Melissa," said Hank, trying to adopt a solemn look to cover up his obvious embarrassment.

"Hi, Melissa!" Gretta cried. "I liked your story. I like kissing and stuff. Hank, let go of my hand. I want to hug her!"

Melissa felt tears form in her eyes as she clutched the child in a close embrace. She'd missed Gretta, especially the loving child she'd first known.

"We haven't seen you in a long time," said the little girl, looking up at her eagerly. "I missed you. I'm sorry about the mushrooms. They weren't really poison, you know."

"I know. I've missed you too," Melissa said while gazing curiously at Hank over Gretta's head. The boy blinked rapidly, then quickly stared down at the floor, rubbing one foot awkwardly against the other. The expression she'd caught in his eyes before he'd looked away had not seemed unfriendly. Could he be here to make amends? she wondered hopefully.

"Can't you come and see us again?" asked Gretta.

Melissa didn't know what to say. The children's appearance had been so sudden. Before she could formulate some kind of answer, Hank broke in.

"Um, you aren't married or anything yet, are you?" he asked in all seriousness, his face turning a brighter red.

Melissa tried not to smile. If Hank was trying to make up, she didn't want to make it too difficult for him. "No, I'm not married yet, Hank."

"Um, good. Then can you come over to our place for dinner tomorrow night?"

"It's a celebration!" exclaimed Gretta, jumping up and down by Melissa's side. "For Christmas!"

"Christmas? In March?"

"It's special," said Hank, finally managing to look his father's girlfriend in the face, his sincere dark eyes reminding her of Rafe. "We're having a dinner with Dad and Gran since we didn't get to celebrate together on the real Christmas Day this year."

"We're havin' turkey and mashed potatoes and everything. Will you come, Melissa? Will you?" Gretta pleaded.

"What does your father say about this?" asked Melissa, still cautious despite her rising excitement. "Maybe I should call him first."

"No!" Hank said hurriedly. "Everyone expects you already. And Dad can't talk right now. He's got laryngitis or something."

"Lip-eye-tus!" Gretta cried.

Hank gave his sister a dirty look. "Yeah. He's got that too. His lips are all swollen up."

"Good heavens!" said Melissa. What a tale! Why weren't they telling the truth? Were the kids trying to surprise their father? What would he do if she showed up on his doorstep? Would he take her in his arms and say he loved her like before? Her heart beat faster at the thought.

"Dad's diseases aren't serious," Hank assured her. "And he'll be able to eat by tomorrow night. Will you come? The dinner's at eight o'clock."

"You're sure I'll be welcome?" Melissa asked, referring as much to the son's attitude toward her as to his father's.

"Yeah, I'm sure," said Hank, averting his eyes. Obviously dealing with another bout of discomfort, he thrust his hands deep into his jacket pockets. "Um, Melissa," he began. "Everybody's . . . sorry if you're mad about anything."

She smiled, realizing Hank was ashamed and sincerely trying to apologize for his former behavior and tricks. At the moment this was probably as close as he could get to being totally honest with her. She didn't want to drive him

175

away by being more direct, so she assured him, "If everybody's truly sorry, I forgive them for . . . anything."

"You do?" Hank was openly relieved. Facing Melissa's bright smile, he even managed a lopsided grin.

"And I'll be happy to come to dinner tomorrow," she said. "At eight o'clock, right? We can all have a good time."

"I have some new software you can look at," Hank offered.

"Sounds like fun." Then, wondering if he would pull away, Melissa reached out to give the boy a hug. She was more than gratified when he shyly hugged her in return.

After Hank and Gretta left, Melissa wandered around the children's reading section, hardly knowing what she was doing. It really happened. Rafe's kids had come to fetch her back to their home—and to their father? She'd thought about calling Rafe ever since their last meeting at Haldan-Northrop, giving various excuses to herself for not getting in touch with him. Now, with Hank's apology, the biggest obstacle to their relationship looked like it could resolve itself. The children wanted to accept her. What had happened to change them? Had Rafe talked to them? Had his attitude toward her changed?

Feeling anticipation one moment and anxiety the next, Melissa walked through the maze of the library's shelving stacks, her mind whirling with questions. Did she have the courage to face Rafe? What would she say? What would he do? Could she forgive him, even if he didn't apologize? Stopping by the reading table, she picked up the knight and dragon fairy tale she'd read and embroidered on that day. Would her own romance have a similar happy ending?

"Yea!" Gretta yelled, bounding up the steps after Hank.

Relaxing in his favorite chair and reading a magazine, Rafe looked up and smiled at the noise his children made as they ran up the stairs to their rooms. They were so excited about the celebration tonight, a belated, traditional Christ-

176

mas dinner to take place on the untraditional night of March 22. Both kids had been buzzing about it for days.

He was still amazed Hank had approached him with the notion. He'd been further surprised when his son had assured him that he and Gretta didn't expect any more presents from him. He'd said they only wanted to have a good time with their Dad and Gran, making up for missing Christmas Day together. What a mature, unselfish idea from a kid.

Could the heart-to-heart talks Rafe had had with his son be having their effect? Hank had listened carefully when his father had talked openly about the divorce and how both parents would continue to love their children. The boy had seemed to understand when Rafe explained that he and Nicole were likely to form other love relationships, possibly even remarry, and that neither parent would choose a new spouse who didn't accept their kids.

He'd then added that Gretta and Hank had to be accepting too. The boy had said nothing to that statement, but had acted as though he were feeling guilty. Would guilt be enough punishment for what his son had done? Rafe wondered, now able to admit the truth. Planning to work up to more concrete talks, Rafe was trying his best to straighten the boy out.

Putting down his magazine, he listened to Louise bustle around in the kitchen and he inhaled the delightful aroma of roasting turkey. He was looking forward to the evening except for one thing—Melissa wouldn't be there to celebrate with them. And, despite his son's involvement in the matter, Rafe knew it was his own fault. He'd thought about calling her or dropping by her apartment many times in the past week, but had never found the nerve. Would she forgive him for the way he'd behaved toward her? For accusing her of unfairly criticizing his children when they'd played tricks on her? For telling her she was immature?

Rafe sighed. Even at the time he'd known he was wrong. He just wouldn't admit it, not even to Louise when she'd confronted him. He'd been the one who'd been immature, thinking only he could understand his children and the pain they'd all gone through because of the divorce. He'd been selfish too. He should have opened up and listened to Melissa long ago. In spite of his outward distrust of her lifestyle, he'd always sensed she was a warm, giving, and trustworthy person.

But he'd been too embarrassed to approach her since he'd seen her at Haldan-Northrop the week before. Later he'd known he'd overreacted. He was positive Melissa and her skinny pal were only friends. But had she really thought she and Rafe could just be friends? That was impossible, considering how he felt about her. He was ready to say he was sorry now. In fact, he was ready to tell her this minute!

And wouldn't you know the kids would want their dinner tonight, the very time he'd found the courage for an apologetic trek over to Melissa's place? Luckily, the dinner wouldn't last all night. He could go over later. Anxiously, Rafe checked his watch and saw it was seven-thirty. Trying not to think about Melissa and get impatient, he rose from the chair and went to the kitchen to see how the dinner was proceeding. On the way he almost collided with Hank, who'd come running back down the stairs.

"We aren't ready to eat yet, Gran," his son said as Louise took a huge roasting pan out of the oven.

"The turkey will dry out if it cooks any longer."

"Aw. Can't we wait for another half hour? That's not so long."

"Aren't you hungry?" Rafe asked, wondering at Hank's unusual behavior.

"Yeah. I just think we should eat at eight o'clock." Hank examined his digital watch. "That's only twenty-two more minutes and six seconds away." The boy paused, furrowing

178

his brow. "Don't you think we could digest the food better if we wait? Otherwise, Gretta might get a stomachache."

Rafe exchanged curious looks with Louise. Why was the boy being so adamant about time, to the point of manufacturing silly excuses? Yet, there was a coiled expectency about Hank, as if his son were excited, that made Rafe keep quiet.

Louise merely shrugged, commenting, "I guess it won't hurt to wait a few minutes. Why don't we put the bird on a platter and you can start carving? I'll dish up the rest of the food. When we're ready to sit it should be about eight o'clock anyway. Hank, you can finish setting the table in the other room with the cloth napkins and the crystal. We might as well be formal."

Slicing white meat from the turkey and carefully removing the drumsticks, Rafe watched Hank go about his task. The boy worked diligently, all the while repeatedly checking his watch. When he was finished with the table Hank paced nervously from room to room. Once the kid even went down to the studio, returning with a disgruntled expression on his face.

"What's the matter with you?" asked Rafe. "Are you expecting Santa Claus in March?"

The boy looked startled. "Uh, no Dad. I feel like wandering around, that's all."

"Hank has a lot of energy, Rafe," said Louise. Did she have a knowing expression on her face? Was she in cahoots with Hank and were they planning a surprise?

At eight o'clock the family seated themselves and Rafe began passing around the heaping plates of food. Red and green candles burned in the middle of the table, surrounded by small evergreen branches, Christmas ornaments, and a few sprigs of real mistletoe Louise had managed to find somewhere.

"Merry Christmas, everyone," Rafe said, holding his

179

wineglass aloft for a toast. "Drink up your soda, kids. You're the ones who wanted this celebration."

Both Gretta and Hank complied, although the little girl was quiet and the boy definitely acted glum. Rafe was about to ask them what was wrong when the doorbell rang.

"I'll get it!" Hank cried, almost knocking his plate off the table as he bolted from his chair.

"I'm gonna help!" shouted Gretta, running after him.

"What in the world are they up to?" Louise asked, echoing her son's unspoken question.

"I'll go see. Maybe they're having something delivered," he said, pushing back his chair.

It was obviously time for the surprise. Grinning to himself as he went to the stairway to peer down, Rafe heard excited whispers below. When he stuck his head farther over the railing, he saw Gretta doing a little dance around a vision in white who glowed almost luminescently in the partial dark of the stairwell. Then he suddenly heard a familiar, tinkling laugh.

He should have recognized her by that sound. Or by the way she glided toward him, lightly ascending the staircase, dressed in an antique beaded dress with wide bell-like sleeves.

But Rafe was expecting a surprise, not a miracle, and he gaped when Melissa raised her sweet, flowerlike face and spotted him at the top of the stairs. Obviously as disconcerted as he, she stood still.

The rest of the scene was magical. Rafe didn't know who moved first. Afterward he only remembered beckoning and reaching out to the shimmering vision, crystal combs sparkling in her soft hair, while she lifted her flowing sleeves and quickly flew up the steps and into his arms. Accepting the enchanting gift, Rafe embraced Melissa with all the fervor of his love and passion.

"Daddy!" complained Gretta. "You're always crushing her wings!"

About to thoroughly kiss his lady, Rafe loosened his hold. In puzzlement he ran his hands over Melissa's back and asked, "What wings?"

Melissa held out an arm and laughed breathlessly. She told Gretta, "These aren't wings, honey. They're just my sleeves."

Louise and Hank had joined the little girl to surround the couple. Melissa and Rafe would have to wait until later for more complete intimacy.

"Surprise! Merry Christmas, Daddy!" Gretta cried, hugging his legs.

"Yeah. Merry Christmas, Dad. We invited Melissa," Hank said proudly, acting as if he were giving Rafe a present.

"I get my very own—" Rafe began.

"Christmas fairy!" interrupted Gretta. "She's the tooth fairy only for me."

"I'll have to remember that," Rafe said dryly.

"Merry Christmas! Happy March 22!" Melissa cried, disengaging Rafe's hold to pull a small bag out from a hidden pocket in her dress. Giggling, she sprinkled everyone and most of the floor around them with sparkling powder.

"Fairy dust!" exclaimed Gretta. "Are we gonna turn into punkins now?"

Hank groaned and poked his little sister.

"It's love magic," said Rafe. Although Melissa was laughing he could tell there were unspoken questions lurking in her bright blue eyes. Quickly taking her in his arms again, he whispered, "I'm sorry. I was such a fool. Can you forgive me?"

"Leave them alone for a minute. Let's go back to the table," said Louise, grabbing Hank and Gretta to lead the reluctant children away. "Did you think of this all by yourselves? I never even guessed. How clever you are!"

Gretta turned as she was dragged off. "Look, Daddy!"

She pointed up at the light fixture above them. "Mistletoe! You're supposed to kiss her!"

"Come on, sweetheart," said Louise, propelling her around the corner.

Rafe didn't need further prompting. He pulled Melissa into the stairwell leading upstairs, trying to get as much privacy as possible in the semiopen area. "Mistletoe magic," he murmured, pressing her tightly against his body, claiming her lips with a long, exploratory kiss. How he needed his little fairy, he thought fiercely. "I'll never let you go again," he whispered before reclaiming her willing mouth.

Her heart warmed by his words, Melissa responded by putting her arms about his neck, oblivious to the way his tight embrace pressed the dress's beading into her breasts. It had been so long since she'd felt this excitement that streaked through her like a shooting star. Their separation had seemed like an eternity. Yet now, anchored once again in Rafe's arms, Melissa felt as if she'd come home.

Without thinking, she gently nipped Rafe's lower lip, sensuously rubbing her body against him.

Groaning, he ran his fevered hands up her sides to possessively cup her breasts. His slight movement backed Melissa gently into the nearby railing of the stairway.

"Oh!" she gasped, suddenly realizing where they were.

"Damn!" he cursed as he relinquished her breasts and looked around him. "We can't do anything here."

"Or in *there*, either. We'll have to wait."

Taking a deep breath and caressing her hair, he gazed deeply into her eyes. "Well, little sugarplum, that's the problem with having children."

"There's only one problem?"

"Well, there are a few others," Rafe admitted sheepishly. "But those are usually caused by parents. Can you find it in your heart to forgive me—and the innocent kids I led wrong? What they did was my fault, you know. I let them get away with too much. And I compared you to Nicole with all her problems. I was so afraid you'd leave me like she did, I couldn't see you as yourself. Then I went and drove you away. Can you believe I loved—love you anyway?"

"I believe you and forgive you. I love you, too, Rafe."

She touched his lips with a kiss as light as gossamer wings, all the time thinking she'd do much more if they were entirely alone.

"I was planning on telling you tonight," he continued between short, sweet kisses. "But the kids planned this dinner, and then you beat me to it."

"Hey, Daddy! Melissa! Are you going to eat or not?" Gretta yelled, sticking her face around the stairwell corner.

"Gretta! Come back here!" Louise shouted.

"We may as well have dinner," Rafe said, then whispered, "I'll make it up to you later!"

Seeing the promise in his penetrating dark eyes, Melissa felt delicious chills climb up and down her spine. It would be difficult to behave during dinner. She would simply have to steel herself to be patient.

As they headed toward the dining room she asked, "Did you know your misguided children came to find me at one of my library jobs, Rafe?" When he shook his head she told him, "They invited me to this dinner. I don't know why or how, but I think they want us to get back together."

"I told you I had great kids!"

When they were seated Louise exclaimed, "What a wonderful dinner this is going to be!"

Sitting beside Melissa, Rafe held her hand tightly, managing to eat with his left hand. Though the food was barely lukewarm, it didn't matter to Melissa. She wasn't hungry anyway. She was satisfied to sit and merely look into Rafe's velvety brown eyes.

"I was afraid our fairy tale wouldn't have a happy ending," she told him.

"So was I."

"What kinda fairy tale are you talking about?" asked Gretta. "I wanna hear it."

"You do?" Rafe turned to the child. "All right. Once upon a time, there was a little fairy who flew over a huge city. She was searching for something. She looked all over as she flew between the spires and the towers of the buildings. The city was beautiful—it shone like gold in the daytime sun and sparkled like it was decorated with strings of diamonds at night. But the fairy kept searching and searching and she couldn't find what she was looking for."

Melissa smiled with delight. She had no idea Rafe was good at storytelling.

"What was the fairy looking for?" asked Gretta, her eyes wide.

"A job in a department store?" questioned Hank jokingly.

"A tooth? Some choc'late candy?" Gretta licked her lips.

"Some friends?" asked Hank.

"No, the fairy was searching for love," declared Louise knowingly.

"That's true." Melissa leaned over the table as she continued Rafe's story. "The fairy was looking for love all right and she found it when she saw the dark prince. She hoped he was looking for her also when she flew down into his arms."

"I hope she didn't knock him over," teased Hank.

"She wasn't flying that fast, dummy!" Gretta hit her brother playfully with a piece of bread.

"Gretta! Don't throw your food around," remonstrated Louise, but the little girl had already retrieved the slice and placed it back on the table.

Rafe's warm breath tickled Melissa's ear, making her shiver. "Am I your dark prince?" he asked gruffly, caress-

184

ing her with his eyes and tickling her knee under the table. "You're definitely my fairy."

"Hey, Daddy! Are you gonna make Melissa our wicket stepmother?" Gretta asked. Everyone stopped eating to stare at the child. "Ow!" Gretta jumped as Hank kicked her under the table. " 'Scuse me! I mean *magical* stepmother, okay?"

Laughing, Rafe told Melissa, "You can take that as an official marriage proposal."

"I accept," she said quickly, the full realization of what she was promising sinking in as she looked around at the family. Not only would she be marrying the man she loved, but she'd be taking on the task of helping him raise his children. Could she do it? Her heart answered a resounding yes.

"Yea!" cried Gretta, waving her spoon and leaping up to hug Melissa. "Can I be the little girl in the wedding that walks around and throws flowers on top of everyone?"

"The flower girl," Louise said. "It's really true? You're going to get married? How wonderful!"

Kissing Gretta and rising to hug Louise and then Hank, Melissa was elated by the family's positive reaction. She sat back down beside Rafe. "We can tell everyone we pledged our troth on Christmas Day. Won't that be romantic?"

"Except it's really March 22," Rafe corrected her.

"So? Holidays are magical. Christmas has no season—just like love," she explained, feeling like her own heart was running over with joy. "You can celebrate a holiday whenever you want. Today is Christmas for me."

"Okay, little Christmas Fairy," he agreed softly. "I only know today's the most wonderful day of my life."

As she gazed into Rafe's beckoning eyes Melissa couldn't wait to be alone with him.

"Come on, kids," said Louise. "Dinner's over. We're going out for dessert so your dad and Melissa can have some time alone. How would you like ice cream in thirty-five

185

different flavors with hot fudge sauce and whipped cream?"

"Whew!" exclaimed Hank. "I'm glad Dad's happy now, but I don't know how much longer I could take the mushy stuff!"

"Then we can go to a movie," Louise added. "Don't worry about the pie I fixed, sweethearts. We can eat it later. Go get your coats."

"I can stay up late tonight? Yea!" cried Gretta. "Merry Christmas!"

"To all," said Hank.

Louise pushed them toward the stairs, but turned to Melissa and Rafe, who were already in each other's arms. Winking, she added, "And to all a good night!"

Catch up with any
Candlelights
you're missing.

Here are the Ecstasies published this past October.

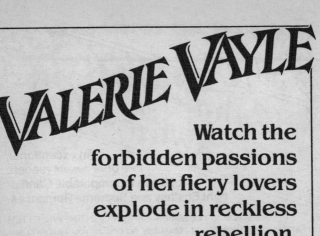

All-new Candlelight Newsletter

An exceptional, *free* offer awaits readers of Dell's incomparable Candlelight Ecstasy and Supreme Romances.

Subscribe to our all-new CANDLELIGHT NEWSLETTER and you will receive—at absolutely no cost to you—exciting, exclusive information about today's finest romance novels and novelists. You'll be part of a select group to receive sneak previews of upcoming Candlelight Romances, well in advance of publication.

You'll also go behind the scenes to "meet" our Ecstasy and Supreme authors, learning firsthand where they get their ideas and how they made it to the top. News of author appearances and events will be detailed, as well. And contributions from the Candlelight editor will give you the inside scoop on how she makes her decisions about what to publish—and how *you* can try your hand at writing an Ecstasy or Supreme.

You'll find all this and more in Dell's CANDLELIGHT NEWSLETTER. And best of all, *it costs you nothing*. That's right! It's Dell's way of thanking our loyal Candlelight readers and of adding another dimension to your reading enjoyment.

Just fill out the coupon below, return it to us, and look forward to receiving the first of many CANDLELIGHT NEWSLETTERS—overflowing with the kind of excitement that only enhances our romances!

DELL READERS SERVICE—DEPT. B881F
P.O. BOX 1000, PINE BROOK, N.J. 07058

Name_____

Address_____

City_____

State_____ Zip_____